The Matrimonial Advertisement

A Holiday By Gaslight

"Matthews (*The Matrimonial Advertisement*) pays homage to Elizabeth Gaskell's *North and South* with her admirable portrayal of the Victorian era's historic advancements...Readers will easily fall for Sophie and Ned in their gaslit surroundings."

— *Library Journal*, starred review

"Matthews' novella is full of comfort and joy—a sweet treat for romance readers that's just in time for Christmas."

— *Kirkus Reviews*

"A graceful love story...and an authentic presentation of the 1860s that reads with the simplicity and visual gusto of a period movie."

— *Readers' Favorite*,
2019 Gold Medal for Holiday Fiction

The Lost Letter

"Lost love letters, lies, and betrayals separate a soldier from the woman he loves in this gripping, emotional Victorian romance...Historical romance fans should snap this one up."

— *Publishers Weekly*, starred review

"A fast and emotionally satisfying read, with two characters finding the happily-ever-after they had understandably given up on. A promising debut."

— *Library Journal*

USA Today Bestselling Author

MIMI MATTHEWS

VICTORIAN ROMANTICS
BOOK 1

FAIR AS A STAR
Victorian Romantics: Book 1
Copyright © 2020 by Mimi Matthews

Edited by Deborah Nemeth
Cover Design by James T. Egan of Bookfly Design
Formatting by Ampersand Book Interiors

E-Book: 978-1-7330569-8-4
Paperback: 978-1-7330569-7-7

"She Dwelt among the Untrodden Ways" by William Wordsworth was originally published in *Lyrical Ballads, with Other Poems*, *Vol. II*, London, T. N. Longman and O. Rees, 1800. It is used in this work by right of public domain.

The Posthumous Papers of the Pickwick Club by Charles Dickens was originally published by Chapman and Hall, London, 1837. It is used in this work by right of public domain.

www.PerfectlyProperPress.com

Dedication

For Stella, Tavi, and Bijou.
And in memory of John, the original untidy little dog.

A violet by a mossy stone
Half hidden from the eye!
—Fair as a star, when only one
Is shining in the sky.

WILLIAM WORDSWORTH
She Dwelt among the Untrodden Ways

Chapter One

Somerset, England
July 1864

*B*eryl Burnham stared out the window of the carriage as it rolled down the narrow country road that ran through the center of Shepton Worthy. Her gaze drifted over the familiar landscape. More than a year had passed since she'd last seen the ancient curving oaks, the rhododendrons rising as high as the cottages they flanked, and the damask roses drooping over low garden walls. Nothing had changed. The village looked as it always had—a veritable pattern card of pastoral perfection.

The only thing that had ever stood out had been Beryl herself.

And now she was home.

It was a suffocating sensation, as much as a joyful one.

What she needed was a moment of fresh air. A chance to stretch her legs, and to break free from the cloying sense of inevitability that had settled over her the moment their train had pulled up to the village's small platform halt.

She lowered the window as the carriage passed the village church. It was a narrow building of worn gray stone, with a Gothic severity to its angles that was belied by the riot of red, blue, and yellow wildflowers that brightened the churchyard, and the soft, fragrant blooms framing the heavy wooden doors.

The *open* doors.

"Stop the coach!" she called out to the driver.

Across from her, Aunt Hortensia was startled from her nap. "What's this?" Her hooded eyes snapped open as the carriage came to a halt. "Have we arrived?"

"Very nearly," Beryl said. "Only another mile."

"Another mile?" Aunt Hortensia withdrew a handkerchief from her beaded reticule to dab at her mouth. She was a stately woman on the other side of sixty who had the unfortunate habit of drooling as she dozed. "Then why have we stopped, pray?"

"It's the church," Beryl said. "The doors are open."

"What on earth does that signify?"

"It means that Mr. Rivenhall is presently inside. I must pay my respects." Beryl was surprised by the urgency of her desire to see him. She and Mark Rivenhall had always been friends. But this was something else. Something different. It coiled tight inside of her. A need so keen that it cut like a knife. As if seeing him would fortify her for what was to come.

And perhaps it might.

Mark had a knack for lifting her spirits. For making her smile, whether in person, or through the many letters he'd written to her during her absence. Sweet, humorous letters. They'd arrived with some regularity, as reliable as Mark was himself. She'd come to depend on those letters. To look for them each week, with as much eager anticipation as a child looking forward to a treat.

"One of the Rivenhall triplets?" Aunt Hortensia gave a scandalized blink. "Most certainly not. You aren't fit to be seen, my girl."

"I look well enough." She was wearing one of the dresses her aunt had purchased for her in Paris. A white cotton day dress, with billowing sleeves and wide flounced skirts trimmed in the same grass-green satin ribbon as the delicate green belt that circled her waist. It was all a bit wrinkled, truth be told, and she'd perspired under the arms a little, but Mark wouldn't care. He was a curate. A man of God. Not the sort to heed such things.

"Nonsense," Aunt Hortensia scoffed. "Mr. Rivenhall is soon to be your brother-in-law. You may call on him after you've bathed and changed from the journey. After you've seen your parents—*and* your betrothed."

"Mr. Rivenhall won't mind." Beryl opened the carriage door before the liveried footman could reach it to assist her. "Go on without me, Aunt. I'll walk the rest of the way home."

Aunt Hortensia's voice rose. "Beryl Elizabeth Burnham—"

"I promise I'll be quick." Beryl permitted the footman to hand her down. "Don't wait for me."

With that, she swung open the rose-festooned church-yard gate—stirring a waft of heady perfume into the sultry summer air—and walked the short distance to the front doors of the church. Voices emanated from within. An elderly lady was complaining loudly. Beryl recognized the distinctive shrill tone. It was one of the village's foremost gossips, Mrs. Doolittle, venting her spleen about her neighbor.

And in response, an equally recognizable deep baritone, uttering a monosyllabic assent here, and a sympathetic murmur there. No one was as understanding as Mark Rivenhall.

He stood with his back to Beryl, his broad shoulders outlined in his cassock, and his seal-brown hair carelessly mussed from too often raking his fingers through it. He was as sweetly familiar to her as Shepton Worthy itself.

The Rivenhall triplets was a name often used to describe the three brothers. But they weren't triplets at all. They'd only been born one year after the other in quick succession. First Henry, now a baronet. And then Jack, a soldier who had tragically met his end last year in Bhutan. And finally, Mark, curate to the current vicar of Shepton Worthy.

"She didn't even apologize," Mrs. Doolittle said. "You see why you must intervene. If you don't, I shall withdraw from the committee. And the fete will be the worse for it, I can promise you—" She broke off abruptly at the sight of Beryl advancing up the nave. "Miss Burnham!"

Mark appeared to still for an instant—in surprise, Beryl hoped—before slowly turning to look at her. The expression in his blue eyes was difficult to read, but the smile that spread over his face was welcoming enough. It was the same ready smile with which he greeted all of his parishioners. "Miss Burnham. I wasn't aware you'd returned."

"Only just. I was passing and saw the doors open. I thought…" Beryl trailed off, feeling all at once the impulsiveness of her gesture. Mark wasn't happy to see her. That was plain enough. His mouth was smiling, but his eyes definitely were not. "Forgive the interruption."

"Not at all. Mrs. Doolittle and I are quite finished."

Mrs. Doolittle looked from Beryl to Mark and back again. She was a petite white-haired lady, clad in unrelieved black crepe. Her eyes were as sharp as a hunting hawk's behind her wire-rimmed spectacles, forever scanning about for fresh morsels of tittle-tattle. "Over a year in Paris," she remarked. "A pleasure trip, I'm told."

"It was." Beryl forced a smile. "My aunt and I had a marvelous time."

Mrs. Doolittle sniffed. "You missed the funeral. But that's none of my business." She inclined her head to Mark. "Mr. Rivenhall. Good day."

"Good day, ma'am."

Beryl bit her tongue until Mrs. Doolittle had exited the church.

"You mustn't mind her," Mark said.

"I never have. I'm not likely to start now."

"No, indeed." He took a step closer to her, only to come to an awkward halt. His fingers pushed through his already disheveled hair, his smile turning a little rueful. "I wish I'd known you were coming."

"Didn't Henry tell you? I mentioned it to him when last I wrote. I'd have written to you as well, but—"

"It wasn't necessary."

"Did you receive my last letter?"

"I did. Thank you."

She came closer to him. "And thank *you*. All of the letters you wrote to me—"

"They were only trifles."

"'Trifles make the sum of life,'" she quoted to him. It was from *David Copperfield*. She and Mark shared a love of Mr. Dickens's novels. It was how they'd first become friends. "Your

5

letters were very welcome. They entertained me to no end. I believe I read the one about Mrs. Jenkins's nephew and the pony a dozen times. It never failed to make me laugh."

"I'm glad I could amuse you."

If Beryl didn't know him better, she might have imagined there was a trace of coolness in his words. She searched his face. "You look well."

"And you…" One hand lifted in a vague gesture, only to fall back to his side. He cleared his throat. "You look—"

"Yes, I know. Rather worse for wear." She gave her rumpled skirts a shake. "Aunt Hortensia warned me not to come in. She said I wasn't fit to be seen. But I had to see you. I wanted to tell you how much I appreciated your letters over the past year, and the fact that you never…you never—"

"What?"

"You never reproached me for not being here for Jack's funeral."

Mark's brows lowered. He took another step toward her. "Has Henry done so?"

"Not in so many words, but I know I disappointed him. I daresay it seemed like I didn't care, leaving as abruptly as I did. I'm afraid he was hurt by my absence."

"Henry will survive. If it's any comfort, he hardly noticed my presence at the funeral, let alone your absence. A year from now he won't remember who was there and who wasn't, nor will any of the villagers."

"I hope you're right."

"Have you seen him yet?" Mark asked.

Beryl shook her head. "I haven't even been home. Aunt Hortensia went ahead with the carriage. I'm to walk the rest of the way to the Grange."

His gaze held hers. "You came here first?"

Warmth crept into her cheeks. "I did." She gave a self-conscious laugh. "I suppose I wanted to see a friendly face before I entered the lion's den."

The strange look in his eyes—so guarded and wary—seemed to soften. "Shall I walk you back?"

Some of the tension in her shoulders eased. "Can you?"

"I'll lock up the church."

"Isn't Mr. Venable about?" Beryl had half expected to see the antiquated vicar. He'd been a fixture at the church ever since she was a girl. A white-haired relic, even then.

"He's confined to his bed. His health has been failing of late. I believe he's finally beginning to seriously contemplate retirement."

"And then you'll be made vicar?"

"That's the idea." Mark's smile dimmed. "It's ultimately up to Henry." He tugged at the front of his cassock. "Will you give me a moment to change?"

"Of course." Beryl waited in the aisle, her gloved hands clasped in front of her. She didn't want to go home. Didn't want to resume the life she'd left a year ago.

Not that Paris had been much better.

There had been more distraction there, certainly. But her secret burden had lurked in the background—through all of her visits to the fashionable shops and her meals at elegant cafés and patisseries—waiting to once again wrap itself around her heart. It wasn't a continuous source of distress, no more than it had been in Shepton Worthy. But it was there. A dark cloud only temporarily eclipsed by the sun.

Mark appeared again in short order, wearing a white linen shirt, with dark woolen trousers and matching waistcoat. His frock coat was draped over his arm.

He wasn't as tall as Henry, nor as brawny as Jack had been—though he still dwarfed Beryl in both height and breadth. But it wasn't his build that made Mark attractive. It was the kindness about him. The sparkle of roguish good humor that made his blue eyes crinkle and his mouth quirk. That humor had been present in all of his letters. Had made her laugh when she felt like weeping.

"Shall we set off?" he asked.

"By all means." She followed him out of the church, waiting on the steps as he locked the doors. "I didn't mean to importune your time."

"Nonsense. I'm glad for the fresh air." He walked alongside her through the churchyard, hands thrust in his pockets. "Glad I was your first stop."

"I thought you were put out."

"Surprised," he admitted. "You took me off of my guard. I hadn't expected you to return until September."

"Yes, well…Aunt Hortensia didn't feel there was any point in staying away any longer. Not with the wedding approaching."

Mark bent his head to conceal a frown. "It is looming ahead, isn't it?"

"Less than three months away." It was impossible not to think of it. Impossible not to contemplate the absolute inevitability of it all. Even in Paris, where she'd been meant to be resting and recovering herself, Aunt Hortensia had insisted that the bulk of their time be spent shopping for Beryl's wedding clothes.

Less than three months.

She was beginning to feel like a prize pig being forced down an increasingly narrow chute.

"October fifteenth," Mark said. "I have it written down in my diary."

As did she. Written down and underlined in heavy pencil. She moistened her lips. "Is Henry much changed?"

"He's been keeping himself busy with estate matters. But that's no different than usual. Truth be told, I haven't seen him very often."

She looked at him. "Why not?"

"I've had too much work to do, what with Mr. Venable being ill, and the villagers needing my input on plans for the summer fete. There have been disputes between some of the ladies about how to proceed this year. Old grievances and such. I've been called upon to play mediator."

"No wonder Mr. Venable has decided to take to his bed."

"Yes, his indisposition is rather convenient. He never did like settling arguments between parishioners, not with any degree of nuance. It was all he could do to make it through the Christmas pageant this year. By the end of it, he was reduced to advising everyone to 'cut the baby in half,' like Solomon."

Beryl laughed. "If only every problem could be solved with such efficiency."

"With an appropriate Bible verse or a meaningful quote from scripture? Venable believes it can."

"You don't, I take it."

"I find it easier to listen to their complaints than to force them to a biblical solution. They only want to be heard."

She looped her arm through his. "And you're a superlative listener."

His muscles tensed at her touch, and then relaxed. "We can't all be baronets or war heroes."

Rays of sunshine shone down through the branches of the oaks that lined the road, filtering through the leaves to warm Beryl's face. "Do you miss him?"

Mark didn't need to ask who she meant. "Every day. Sometimes, when something humorous happens in the village, I still have the urge to write to him. I have to remind myself that he's gone."

She squeezed his arm. "I'm sorry I wasn't here for you."

"For Henry, you mean."

"For both of you. I'm afraid I haven't been a very good friend. I've been selfish. Absent when you most—" She stopped herself. There was no point in self-recrimination. "But I mean to remedy that. From now on, I'm completely at your service. Anything you require of me, you need only ask."

"Anything?" He smiled.

"So long as my mother and Henry can spare me. I don't mean to be idle."

"You never were."

"No," she said. "Only restless."

He touched the back of her gloved hand as it curled around his arm. His fingers brushed over the small whitework figure she'd stitched into the fabric. "Is this one of your own designs?"

"It is."

"A dragonfly?"

"A damselfly." She'd worked on it in the evenings during her final weeks in Paris. The thread had been chosen with care to perfectly match her gloves, each stitch placed with faithful intention. "They were often flitting about near the Seine. I was able to sketch some images to work from."

He traced the embroidery. "Hiding in plain sight."

"That's the beauty of whitework. It's never ostentatious." It was her favorite form of embroidery, white thread on matching white fabric. She liked to place small figures on the corner of a linen handkerchief or the hemmed cuff of a cambric undersleeve. Secret stitches that hid in plain sight, just as Mark had said. The sort that were discovered unexpectedly, and that gave the finder an instant of surprised delight.

He looked at her. "You have a formidable talent."

Her mouth tilted up at one corner. "For whitework."

"Don't be dismissive of it."

"I'm not. I only dispute what you call it. *A formidable talent.* As if there's anything particularly formidable about embroidery. It's a ladies' pastime, that's all. Something to fill the empty hours. It has no real worth outside of a moment's pleasure in looking at it."

"It gives you pleasure, doesn't it? The hours you spend in creating it? That alone makes it a thing of value."

She privately conceded his point. Her whitework embroidery did have value to her. It steadied her mind, and gave her the means to be creative. To exercise a skill which she imagined to be similar to that of a miniature portrait painter, albeit with a needle and thread.

"You gave me an embroidered handkerchief once," he said. "Do you remember?"

"Of course." She'd given one to Henry as well. It had been years ago. A small Christmas gift to each of them. "I'm surprised that *you* do."

"I still have it."

Her eyes met his. "Do you?"

"Naturally," he said. "It's one of my treasures."

Heat rose in her cheeks. "Nonsense."

"It is." A glint of humor shone in his gaze. "Do you know, I rather envy my brother. He has a lifetime of such artfully stitched linens to look forward to. Nearly invisible dragonflies and damselflies and whatever other insects take your fancy."

"Insects. Really. I do occasionally stitch other things."

"Such as? I can only recall ladybirds and centipedes—"

"I've never embroidered a centipede in my life."

"Caterpillars, then."

She failed to suppress a smile. "It was butterflies, you wretch. As well you know."

He flashed her a grin. "Ah, yes. Quite right. I expect you've given them up, now that you've turned your attention to damselflies."

"No, indeed. Butterflies are still my favorite subjects." She was endlessly fascinated by their delicate majesty. By their wings, as colorfully patterned as the stained-glass windows in a great cathedral.

But it was more than that.

"I like things that change into other things," she said. "That have the ability to transform into something beautiful."

"Everything you stitch is beautiful," he said.

The compliment filled Beryl with a warm glow. Despite her protestations, she took pride in her whitework. His recognition of it meant the world to her. "You're very kind to say so."

"It's the truth, merely."

Up ahead, the road split in two at the trunk of an enormous oak. The Grange was to the left, Rivenhall Park to the right.

She and Mark came to a halt.

There was no more point in delaying. It was time to go home. To see her mother and sister, and to face her future with

Henry. Beryl no longer felt suffocated by the prospect. Being with Mark had given her room to breathe, just as it always did.

"I'd best go the rest of the way on my own." She slid her arm from his. "Thank you for accompanying me this far."

"Will I see you again?" he asked.

"Undoubtedly. In church on Sunday, if not before." On impulse, she stretched up to press a brief, grateful kiss to his cheek. "Goodbye for now."

He didn't say anything. Didn't move or even seem to breathe. As she turned away from him to walk down the left branch of the road, she had the strange sense he was still standing where she'd left him. Frozen to the spot, watching her.

She didn't look back to find out.

Mark entered the library at Rivenhall Park, shutting the door behind him. The dark wood-paneled room was unchanged from his father's time. Bookcases laden with heavy leather-bound volumes still lined the walls, and a rich red-and-gold Aubusson carpet still covered the floor. The faint residue of pipe-smoke lingered in the air. Father's favorite blend. And at the opposite end of the room, in lonely splendor, was a mahogany desk of truly magnificent proportions. Father's desk.

But not anymore.

Behind it, his head bent over a ledger, sat Mark's older brother, Henry.

Sir Henry, now.

He looked so much like their father that Mark almost recoiled. But he was no longer a lad. He was a man of thirty.

A sensible clergyman who had long since ceased being intimidated by his brother's granite exterior.

Crossing the room, he came to stand in front of the desk. He saw no utility in mincing words. "I've just encountered Miss Burnham."

Henry's quill stilled in his hand. He slowly raised his head. His eyes registered no surprise at Mark's revelation. "Oh?"

"Why didn't you tell me she was coming home early?"

His brother's expression was as implacable as his words. "Why do you think?"

Mark inwardly winced. Henry was many things, but he was no fool. "You might have done. I'd have liked to prepare myself for the shock."

"Was it a shock? You must have known she'd return eventually." Setting aside his quill. Henry leaned back in his chair. "Oh, do sit down, Mark. I don't care for you looming over me."

Mark grudgingly sank into one of the leather-upholstered chairs facing the desk. They were usually occupied by Henry's subordinates. Those petitioning for his help or—more often—his funds.

"Where is she now?" Henry asked.

"Gone home. I expect she'll send a note round to you when she gets there."

"Her mother will, at least. Mrs. Burnham is nothing if not obliging." Henry rubbed a hand over the side of his face. There were deep lines etched around his mouth and at the corners of his eyes that hadn't been present a year ago. Evidence of overwork and too many days consumed with grief after news had come of Jack's death in Bhutan. "They'll no doubt invite me to dine."

"Well," Mark said, "consider yourself warned."

"I'm obliged to you." Henry stood, pushing his chair out behind him. "Would you care for a glass of brandy?"

"No, thank you." It hadn't escaped Mark that, the moment he sat down, Henry rose. His brother didn't care much for being loomed over, but he rather enjoyed doing the looming.

"Suit yourself." Henry went to his drinks table and poured himself a measure from the crystal decanter on the tray. He drank it down in one swallow. "How did she look?"

Exceedingly dear.

"Fashionable," Mark said.

Henry refilled his glass. "I suppose that's to be expected after a year in Paris."

Mark refrained from commenting. It hadn't been a lie. He *had* noticed that Beryl appeared to be more fashionably turned out.

But that hadn't been all he'd noticed.

Her honey-blond hair was streaked golden from the sun, and the bridge of her nose lightly dusted with freckles. She'd been outdoors while she was away. A great deal of the time, if he was to guess. She looked healthy, but…she hadn't looked entirely well.

There had been a vulnerability in her countenance. A hint of some hidden worry Mark couldn't quite put his finger on. But he'd recognized it all the same. Indeed, when she'd drawn back from kissing him, her wide blue-green eyes had seemed a bit sad somehow. A bit lost.

It was the same vulnerability he'd glimpsed in her face a year ago, on the day before she'd left Shepton Worthy without saying goodbye.

He'd wanted to reach out to her. To ask her what was wrong. Instead, he'd just stood there, utterly flummoxed by the sensation of her pillow-soft lips brushing his cheek.

She'd never kissed him before, not in all the years he'd known her. Not even so much as a friendly peck.

Which was all this had been.

A kiss any young lady might have bestowed on a future brother-in-law. It didn't mean anything. He reminded himself of that fact for what felt like the hundredth time.

"Her aunt will have purchased her wedding clothes there," Henry said, taking another drink of brandy.

"I really have no idea."

"The subject never came up in any of the letters the two of you exchanged?"

Mark's gaze narrowed. "You make it sound as though we were in constant correspondence."

"Weren't you? I know you wrote to her regularly."

"I relayed entertaining anecdotes about the village. About my parishioners and their children." Mark stood. He was in no mood to argue with his brother. "Speaking of which, I'd best get back to them."

Henry sloshed his brandy in his glass. "You may well be invited to dinner this evening, too."

"You can rest easy. I'm not likely to accept." Mark walked to the door. As he reached to open it, a haphazard flower arrangement on a low table caught his eye. It was wildflowers—an entire porcelain vase spilling over with them. He wondered that he hadn't noticed it before. "Mrs. Guthrie's tastes have changed since last I visited."

Rivenhall Park's rather despotic housekeeper wasn't known for frivolity. A dignified arrangement of roses was her preferred decoration, and that in the drawing or dining room—never in the library.

Henry cast a brief look at the wildflowers. His mouth twisted into a dry smile. "That's not Mrs. Guthrie's doing. Those came from Miss Winnifred. She brought them this morning when she came to go riding."

Winnifred Burnham was Beryl's younger sister. She had the dubious distinction of being the village's most eligible young lady. She was also unrepentantly horse mad. As a girl, she'd been a regular fixture at the Rivenhall Park stables.

"Is she here often?"

"More than usual of late," Henry said. "I've given her leave to exercise that stallion I bought at the sales. She has a way with the brute."

Mark frowned. Winnifred was a capable enough horsewoman when mounted on a sensible mare or a gelding, but stallions were something else altogether. They could be dangerously unpredictable. "Her mother approves?"

"I don't believe she knows of it. Thus far, Miss Winnifred has restricted her riding to the Park."

Mark's frown deepened. It wasn't like Henry to be so careless. "You'd better pray no harm comes to the girl."

"Is that a warning, little brother?" Something dark flickered at the back of Henry's gaze. "Shall I give you one in return? Or is that particular warning, perhaps, better left unsaid?"

Mark's expression hardened. He didn't dignify his brother's word with a reply. Settling his hat back on his head, he exited the library, shutting the door behind him.

Chapter Two

"Oh, my heavens!" Winnifred lifted an elegant Worth and Bobergh evening gown of pale blue silk taffeta from its tissue-paper wrappings. "The fabric feels divine. And is that an interchangeable bodice? Great goodness. It has mother-of-pearl buttons. Yes, I do believe this is my favorite of all your new dresses."

Beryl glanced up from her embroidery. She was seated in the window embrasure, one of her new white cotton petticoats draped across her lap. A honeybee was slowly taking shape at the hem, stitched in white floss. "That's what you said about the last one."

Her sister shot her an impatient look. "Well, how was I to know you'd have an actual Worth evening gown packed in your trunk? You never said so in your letters."

"I believe I did."

"You only mentioned Mr. Worth designing your wedding dress. You said nothing about Aunt Hortensia having purchased an evening gown for you. And you certainly didn't mention that you'd be bringing it home with you in your trunk."

"It must have slipped my mind." Unlike Beryl's wedding dress, which was to be shipped separately from Paris, the evening gown had been ready at the time she and Aunt Hortensia had departed.

"Really, Beryl. If I had an evening gown designed by Empress Eugénie's own dressmaker, you can be sure everyone would know it."

Winnifred moved to the gilt-framed pier glass that stood opposite Beryl's carved four-poster bed. Holding the evening gown up over her rumpled riding habit, she posed this way and that, admiring her reflection. "Aunt Hortensia should have taken me to Paris, not you."

"Yes, she should have," Beryl agreed.

Winnifred was unmollified. "I knew you wouldn't enjoy it. And if you were going to be miserable regardless, I don't see why you couldn't have been miserable in Shepton Worthy. I'd have been happy in Paris. I'd have taken full advantage of Aunt's generosity. Only think of the riding costumes I might have had made there."

Beryl didn't imagine that her sister expected a reply. She turned her attention back to her whitework. No sooner had she done so than the door to her bedroom opened again.

"There you are," Mama said, frowning at Winnifred. "Haven't you heard me calling for you?"

"Look, Mama." Winnifred turned to face her mother, still holding up the gown. "It's a genuine Worth. Have you ever seen anything like it?"

"Stop wrinkling the fabric, my dear. Give it to Mary so she can press it for this evening." Mama entered the room, a folded piece of notepaper in her hand. She was wearing an apron over her dress. She often did when working in her garden. "I've just heard from Sir Henry. He'll be dining with us tonight." She urged Winnifred to the door. "Go and choose a dress to wear from your wardrobe. Mary must have ample time to sponge and press it. I'll have no last-minute scrambling to remove old stains from the stables."

"Must you always bring that up? It only happened once."

"Once was more than sufficient," Mama said. "Off with you!"

With a sigh, and a muttered "yes, Mama," Winnifred exited Beryl's room.

Mama turned to Beryl, her expression transforming into one of artificial cheer. At fifty years of age, she was still an acknowledged beauty, with her silvery blond hair and delicate features. Indeed, she and Winnifred resembled each other to an extraordinary degree. "Are you excited to see Sir Henry again?" she asked.

"Not excited, no. But it will be nice to see him. It's been a long while."

"And you won't be glum, will you, my dear? We're all done with that, aren't we?"

Beryl forced a smile. It felt embarrassingly unnatural. A mockery of a smile, really. Inauthentic and brittle as glass. "I'm done with being glum."

"Good girl." Her mother was visibly relieved. "I prayed a holiday would do the trick. Hortensia was persuaded that all you required was a change. Never mind what that medical journal of Mr. Cooper's advised."

"You needn't speak of that."

"No, indeed. The vile thing. I'm glad you disposed of it."

Beryl briefly looked away, unable to meet her mother's eyes. The village surgeon, Mr. Cooper, had given Mama his copy of the *Provincial Medical and Surgical Gazette* last year. After reading the pages he'd marked, Mama had commanded Beryl to burn it. And Beryl had meant to. She really had. But when it came to the point, she'd been unable to do so.

The vile thing was presently tucked beneath Beryl's mattress, its pages worn from reading and rereading.

"Your aunt and I knew what was best for you all along, didn't we?" Mama beamed. "I won't make light of things. I realize it's been difficult, but—"

"It's fine, Mama," Beryl said. "I'm fine."

"I'm glad to hear you say so, darling. What a weight it's been on my mind. And keeping it all a secret...well. It was necessary, I daresay."

Beryl studied her mother's face. "*Did* you keep it secret?"

Mama wandered to Beryl's dressing table, idly straightening the silver-plated hairbrush set and cut-crystal bottle of elderflower water that adorned its polished walnut surface. "I may have mentioned a few of the details to Mr. Venable."

"Mama!" Beryl's embroidery slipped from her hands. "How could you? You promised me—"

"He's the vicar. It's his job to condole with his flock during difficult times. To be sure, he was quite a good listener, though he understands what ails you no more than I do." Abandoning the dressing table, Mama came to sit down beside Beryl in the window. She slipped a slim arm around her shoulders. "Oh, don't look so stricken. Mr. Venable won't tell anyone. The confessional is sacrosanct."

"We're not papists, Mama."

"No, but—"

"And the confidentiality of the confessional wouldn't have stopped Mr. Venable from confiding in a fellow clergyman. He'll have told Mark Rivenhall everything."

"I'm sure he would do no such thing. And even if he had, what does it matter? Mr. Rivenhall is a curate. He won't go spreading tales to Henry, if that's what you're concerned about."

No. Mark wouldn't spread tales at all. But that was entirely beside the point. The fact was, Mark *knew*. He must have known. No wonder he'd acted so strangely when she'd gone to see him at the church. No wonder he'd looked at her, not like a friend, but like a—

She didn't know what.

It was only later, as he'd walked her home, that he'd attempted to jolly her. An afterthought, no doubt. She was embarrassed to think of how she'd laughed. How she'd relaxed into their friendship as if nothing had changed.

"That's all behind us," Mama said. "All that unpleasantness. You'll bathe and Mary will arrange your hair and you'll put on that beautiful dress…" She squeezed Beryl's shoulders. "Yes, all will be well. You shall see, my love." She kissed Beryl's cheek before rising and walking to the door. "Remember, no more gloom!"

As the door shut, Beryl leaned her head against the window. Outside, the leaves on the trees fluttered lazily in the afternoon breeze. Mama's gardening basket and tools sat on the ground near the rosebushes, abandoned when Henry's note had arrived from Rivenhall Park. Mama wanted nothing more than to see both of her daughters happily married.

She'd been widowed early in her own marriage, not long after Winnifred was born. Fortunately, her jointure had been generous enough to keep them in relative comfort, first at the family estate in Cornwall—until a distant cousin formally took up residence—and now at the Grange. They had no real luxuries to speak of, but there was little about which to legitimately complain. Mama was happy as she was, and would be happier still when Beryl and Sir Henry were married. And if Winnifred were to swiftly follow suit—to marry some lord or sir—Mama's happiness would be complete.

Beryl felt guilty for being so difficult. She was soon to be Lady Rivenhall. A lofty title, to be sure. Only think of the good she might do. She should be effervescent. It wasn't as if she was betrothed to a villain in a fairy tale. Henry was no ogre. He was handsome and honorable, albeit a little too somber on occasion. More importantly, she'd known him since she was fifteen. He was familiar to her. Comfortable.

His proposal last year hadn't surprised her. And her acceptance hadn't surprised him. Their future together had long been assured. Not because they were in love, or because of some passionate infatuation, but because they suited each other. Henry had seen that. It's why he'd courted her. He'd recognized that she had the qualities necessary to make him a good wife.

She'd recognized it, too. It was the reason she'd accepted him. Why she'd been pragmatic instead of romantic. She'd thought only in terms of compatibility. It had seemed enough. A marriage built on friendship and mutual respect. A union that would see her and her family well taken care of. Such a match was beneficial to everyone.

Why then did she find it so difficult to smile? To show any excitement over the plans for her wedding? No one had forced her to accept Henry. It had been her own decision, made in full possession of her wits.

Now, all that was left was to get up and get on with it.

Rousing herself from the window, she withdrew to the bath where she soaked in a rose-oil infused tub and washed her hair with eggs that had been beaten to a cream. Once Beryl's hair was dry, Mary—the lady's maid Beryl shared with her mother and sister—arranged Beryl's thick tresses in a roll at her nape, securing it with a dozen hairpins and a matching set of lapis lazuli combs. Set on a background of gold, the glossy bluish-purple stones glimmered in the lamplight as Beryl at last stepped in to the voluminous silk taffeta skirts of her evening dress.

"Will you be wanting the evening bodice?" Mary asked.

"The day bodice." The short, ruffled sleeves and low neckline of the evening bodice were better suited to a ball than a dinner at home. Mama might disagree, but Beryl felt no need to be so much on display. Not for Henry's sake.

Mary helped her into the long-sleeved bodice, with its mother-of-pearl buttons and delicate silk belt. It fit as snugly as a custom-made kid glove.

Beryl set a hand at her waist. "It's very tight."

"Shall I cinch your corset another half inch?"

"No, no." Beryl gave her a fleeting smile. "I shall just have to remember not to eat too much."

Later, sitting in the drawing room with her mother, sister, and aunt, Beryl awaited the arrival of Sir Henry. Like most of the reception rooms at the Grange, the drawing room was elegant enough on its surface. However, looking with a critical eye, one could easily discern that the paper hangings were faded in places, the Turkish carpet singed near the fireplace, and the sofa and chairs in need of reupholstering.

Mama made do the best she could. She hadn't much choice. Aunt Hortensia's generosity never stretched to redecorating. A Londoner herself, she couldn't see the sense in it. The

Grange was a country house—far removed from fashionable society—and only theirs on lease.

"Pity Mr. Rivenhall was unable to join us," Mama said. "We still wouldn't have had even numbers, but it might have been less obvious."

Beryl's gaze jerked to her mother. "He couldn't come?"

"He sent his regrets. I suppose he's busy at church this evening, what with Mr. Venable ill. The poor fellow is stricken with a wasting disease. He hasn't long, I gather."

"Haven't you any other neighbors you could have invited, Griselda?" Aunt Hortensia asked. "A gentleman for Winnifred? Or for yourself?"

Mama's cheeks turned pink. "Really, Hortensia."

"And why shouldn't I matchmake for you?" Aunt Hortensia asked. "You've been widowed nearly twenty years. It's high time you remarried."

"You've been widowed twice as long, Aunt," Winnifred pointed out.

Aunt Hortensia was the eldest sister of Beryl's late father. A reputed beauty in her youth, she'd married early and well, only to be widowed within a year. On his death, her husband—Mr. Sheldrake—had left her the entirety of his vast fortune.

"That's different, my girl. A wealthy widow has no cause to remarry. While a lady in your mother's circumstances has every reason to do so."

"It doesn't matter anyway," Winnifred said. "There are no eligible gentlemen hereabouts. No one save Sir Henry and Mr. Rivenhall. And Simon Black, of course, but who would invite him anywhere?"

"Simon Black?" Aunt Hortensia raised her filigree lorgnette to her eyes to better examine Mama's face.

"He's the new doctor," Mama said. "A proper physician, and a rather singular one at that. He arrived three months ago when old Mr. Cooper retired to Bath."

Beryl stilled. "You didn't tell me that Mr. Cooper had gone."

Mama gave Beryl a blank look. "Should I have mentioned it? It seemed of no account."

"I'd like to have known." It would have been a decided weight off of Beryl's mind. She'd been plagued with worry over running into Mr. Cooper again ever since she'd left Paris. At the time, she'd believed he was the only one—outside of Mama and Aunt Hortensia—who knew the truth of why she'd left Shepton Worthy so abruptly last year. Indeed, if not for Aunt Hortensia's intervention, Mama might have taken Mr. Cooper's terrible advice on the subject.

And then where would Beryl be? Not at home, certainly. Not at liberty.

But now he was gone, that wretched man. She should be relieved. Overjoyed. And yet...

How could she be? Mr. Cooper might be gone, but Mr. Venable was still here. Mark was still here. And they both knew everything.

Everything.

The very thought of it depressed her spirits to an extraordinary degree.

"Yes, yes," Aunt Hortensia interrupted impatiently. "But why didn't you invite this Dr. Black? If he's the new physician—"

"We hardly know the fellow," Mama said. "It would have made little sense to extend an invitation."

Winnifred opened her painted-paper fan. "I've met him on several occasions, and I don't like him at all. He's an aggravating man, with no respect for tradition."

Aunt Hortensia turned her lorgnette on Winnifred. "Since when do you concern yourself with tradition, my girl?"

"That's different. I may flout the rules, but Dr. Black doesn't acknowledge them at all. He's a revolutionary, intent on dismantling the aristocracy."

"I doubt that very much, my dear," Mama said.

Their aged footman, Wilmot, stepped into the drawing room. "Sir Henry Rivenhall," he announced in stentorian tones.

Sir Henry entered an instant later. He was a strikingly handsome man, with the same dark hair and blue eyes possessed by his younger brother. Only two years older in fact, his gaze was ages older in experience. After his father's death over a decade ago, he'd single-handedly brought the Rivenhall Estates back from the brink of bankruptcy, managing to pay off his father's debts and make a fortune in the bargain. The stress of it had taken its toll.

Indeed, he looked even older than Beryl remembered. It was no doubt a result of losing Jack. Henry had always been closest with his middle brother.

His gaze lit on her the moment he walked into the room. He bowed to them in greeting, acknowledging her mother and aunt before gracing Beryl with a slight smile. There was no particular warmth in it. No more, she suspected, than was in her own

She extended her hand to him. "It's good to see you, Henry."

"Beryl." He pressed a kiss to her knuckles. "Paris agreed with you, I see."

"Doesn't she look beautiful?" Mama asked. "A sight for sore eyes, that's what I call her."

"She's had too much sun," Aunt Hortensia said. "When you take her out, sir, you must see she remembers her parasol."

"Indeed," Henry said. "I'm eager to start looking after her." Releasing Beryl's hand, he took a seat beside her on the settee. He was clad in evening black, with a light-colored satin waistcoat and cravat.

"We haven't many weeks to wait until the wedding," Mama continued brightly. "Though it can't happen soon enough for my taste. I shall be grieved to lose my daughter, naturally, but the pair of you have waited long enough, I feel."

Henry smiled at Beryl's mother. "My sentiments exactly, ma'am."

Beryl's own smile remained firmly on her face through dinner. By the time they all returned to the drawing room for coffee, her cheeks were aching. No one seemed to notice. Mama, Winnifred, and Aunt Hortensia were too busy discussing wedding plans and the fast-approaching summer fete. It was Henry who finally put a stop to the conversation by the simple expedient of rising from his chair.

"It's a fine evening," he said to Beryl. "Will you walk with me awhile in the garden?"

"Oh yes, do," Mama encouraged her.

Beryl stood, and taking Henry's arm, accompanied him through the glass doors that led out onto the terrace, and down the steps to the garden.

"It smells like a perfumery," Henry remarked as they crossed the lawn.

"Mama does love her roses." They were the crowning jewel of the Grange's garden, each bush perfectly manicured, and every bloom in the peak of health. Leaf mold and white-flies weren't allowed within an inch of the place, and weeds daren't show their scraggly faces. A gentle lady in every other respect, Mama was absolutely ruthless when it came to protecting her flowers.

Henry steered Beryl onto the flagstone path. It was flanked with torches, recently lit for the evening. "You don't share her passion?"

"I don't, I'm afraid." She cast him an apologetic glance. "Why? Were you imagining I had an affinity for gardening?"

"Not at all. My groundskeeper and gardener do well enough without feminine intervention. Still…" Henry seemed to weigh his words with greater than usual care. "I'd hoped you might find something to interest you at the Park. Some little hobby to occupy your time."

Beryl's smile faltered. She recognized what he was about. He was managing her. *Attempting* to manage her. Just as he managed everything else in his world. She usually didn't mind it. But tonight, for some reason, it grated.

Some little hobby.

Could he be any more patronizing?

Her whitework was her hobby—her passion. Henry would know that if he troubled to know her at all.

"We won't be able to get away from Shepton Worthy anytime soon," he went on. "Not with the harvest coming in."

"I didn't expect we would."

"But you enjoy traveling. You require diversion."

She gave him a long look. "Is this about Paris?"

"It *was* a surprise. You going away so abruptly, and for such a length of time."

"For me as well. I hadn't any notion that Aunt Hortensia would invite me to accompany her, or that I'd need to make up my mind so quickly."

"You might have declined her invitation."

"And risk upsetting her? I couldn't have. Not with Mama and Winnifred to consider. You know we're dependent on my aunt's generosity. And after you and I marry—"

"There's been talk." Henry's voice was peculiarly flat.

A knot formed in Beryl's stomach. She nevertheless endeavored to keep her own voice light. "What kind of talk?"

"Scurrilous gossip about why you left so suddenly. Why you didn't stay for Jack's funeral. I won't repeat it."

"I wish you would."

"I'd not have mentioned it at all except that I'd rather you were prepared for it."

"I'm prepared. One can't have lived here as long as my family has and not be."

It was an unpleasant truth. Shepton Worthy may have been the prettiest village for miles around, but there was a wealth of ugliness beneath its damask-rosebud surface. Like most small villages, it was a hotbed of gossip and scandal, especially during those periods of the year when social activities were at a lull. Indeed, in the long months between the Christmas pageant and the summer fete, there was little else to occupy the residents save spreading gleeful reports of the various peccadilloes of their neighbors.

Beryl wasn't entirely surprised that she'd fallen victim to it. She was, after all, marrying Sir Henry Rivenhall, the most sought-after matrimonial prize in the county. Add to that her sudden departure for Paris, and the gossip fairly created itself.

"Be that as it may, I don't care to have your name bandied about." Henry paused before adding, "Nor mine."

The knot in her stomach tightened. He was reprimanding her in a typically Henry way. Warning her that her behavior had reflected badly upon his good name.

Her behavior.

Good gracious, if he only knew.

She felt vaguely ill at the thought of it all. "Henry, I—"

"Beryl!" Winnifred strode toward them across the lawn, an Indian shawl in one hand and her flounced skirts clutched in another. "I've brought you your wrap. Mama says it's getting cooler and that you mustn't take a chill so close to your wedding day."

Beryl accepted it without a word, drawing the soft cashmere around her shoulders. It was only a shawl, but at the moment it struck her as a suffocating symbol of all of Mama's hopes for her future. An unwelcome reminder that, if Beryl took ill again, she'd dash those hopes. Not just for Mama, but for Winnifred too, whose future depended so very much on Beryl's own.

"Very thoughtful," Henry said. "But where is yours?"

"Oh, I don't need one," Winnifred replied carelessly. "I'm as healthy as a horse." Her gaze turned acquisitive. "Speaking of which…did you tell Beryl about Vesper?"

"Vesper?" Beryl looked from Winnifred to Henry.

"A stallion I bought while you were away," Henry said. "Your sister has been exercising him for me."

"More than that. I've developed a bond with him. An affinity. He doesn't care for any of Sir Henry's grooms, but when he sees me, he always—"

"I beg your pardon," Henry said. "It grows late, and I still have business to attend to at the Park. If you'll excuse me?"

"Of course," Beryl said.

He took her hand briefly once more and pressed another kiss to it. She supposed the touch of his lips should have made her pulse leap or her heart flutter. It did neither. She felt absolutely nothing. Nothing when he kissed her hand. Nothing when he made them a curt bow, and took his leave.

She watched him depart, neither regretful, nor relieved. Merely…empty.

"Well!" Winnifred huffed. "The least he could have done was allow me to finish my sentence. I expect he'd have let you do so, had you made more than a peep."

"About your horse? How could I? I only just learned of the creature."

"He's not *my* horse," Winnifred said. "I'm destined to have none of the things I want. Not Vesper. Not a Worth gown. If Aunt Hortensia had decided to make me her pet last year instead of you, then perhaps I—" She broke off, her shoulders sagging. "I'm sorry. I don't mean to be a Jealous Jenny."

"You're not a Jealous Jenny." Beryl linked her arm through her sister's. "You're a Willful Winnie. You always have been."

"It did hurt to be left behind. I so desperately wanted to go with you."

"I know, dearest. But you wouldn't have enjoyed it as much as you imagine. You and Aunt Hortensia are like oil and water."

"Were you always in her company?" Winnifred asked. "Every minute of the day?"

"And well into the evening, too," Beryl said. Her aunt had been disposed to keep a close eye on her.

"How tedious. Still, I think I might have endured it. Especially if there was a new wardrobe weighing in the balance. I adore beautiful things."

"Naturally."

"And you're not to think it's because I have some addle-brained notion of catching myself a husband. I won't end my youth as an ornament on some gentleman's mantelshelf. I should wither if I was consigned to such a life. I should die."

Beryl was surprised by her sister's adamance. "What *do* you want out of life?"

"Recognition," Winnifred said without hesitation. "I want to ride the fastest, and row the hardest. I want to be the best—and to have everyone know I'm the best. As good as a man, anyway. I can't stand being condescended to."

"You sound as though you're speaking of someone specific. Has a particular gentleman been condescending to you?"

Winnifred fidgeted with one of the silk bows on her over-skirt. She didn't answer, asking instead, "Don't you bristle at it, Beryl? At always being treated as if you were a child, merely on account of having been born a woman?"

"I don't much care for it, no, but I can't say I let it distress me."

"Because you're already distressed."

Beryl didn't reply. There was no need. Winnifred scarcely stopped for breath.

"Can you find nothing to bring you joy?"

"Many things bring me joy."

"If that were true, you wouldn't have gone away. I still can't understand why you did. Unless… Was it because of Sir Henry? Have you fallen out of love with him?"

Beryl let her gaze drift over the garden. Unfocused. Unseeing. "No. It's not that."

"I wouldn't blame you if you had. He's an infuriating beast at times. Did you know, he insists I take a groom with me when I ride Vesper? Even within the Park? I declare, he thinks he's our father."

"Not mine, I trust."

FAIR AS A STAR

"No, that would be rather awkward, wouldn't it? But he presumes to act as my father. And I don't care for it at all."

"Shall I speak to him about it?"

"Don't you dare. I'll not have him learn that he's managed to ruffle my feathers. It is *I* who mean to ruffle *him*. If you must know, the two of us are engaged in a private war. So private he's not even aware of it. But I mean to win all the same."

A smile quirked Beryl's mouth. It was a genuine one this time. "Have a care how you wage your battles. Henry's good humor only stretches so far." Her smile dimmed. "Speaking of which…"

"Yes?"

"You haven't heard any gossip about me, have you? About why I left the village?"

Winnifred affected a high degree of interest in the trimmings on her skirts. "What sort of gossip?"

"The unpleasant variety."

"Oh, that." Winnifred fell quiet for a moment. "I don't give any credit to it. If you'd done something wrong—something scandalous—I'd know about it, wouldn't I?"

"What are they saying?" Beryl asked.

"It's rather malicious."

Beryl's stomach turned over on itself. "Go on. I want to know."

"Very well." Winnifred inhaled a deep breath, as if steeling herself to deliver bad news. "The prevailing rumor is that you went away to have a baby."

"*A baby?*" Beryl's arm slid nervelessly from her sister's.

"And that isn't the half of it. There are some in the village who've suggested that Jack Rivenhall was the father. They say that's why you missed his funeral. That you were distraught because you'd been having a secret love affair with him, and had been left unmarried and with child."

Beryl's knees went weak. It was all she could do to keep walking. "How do they imagine any of that could have happened with Jack away soldiering for two years or more?"

"Lord knows. I didn't say it was reliable gossip. Just malicious." Winnifred's finely arched brows snapped together in a scowl. "And now you've gone pale." She drew Beryl to a stone garden bench tucked beneath a nearby rose arbor. "Come. You'd best sit down before you faint."

Beryl sank onto the bench without protest. She was almost afraid to ask. "Is that the worst of it?"

"That you cuckolded Sir Henry with his own dead brother?" Winnifred took a seat beside her. "How could it be any worse?"

It could be the truth, that's how.

But Beryl couldn't give voice to her fears. "You're right. It's quite bad enough. I must make an effort to quell it, for everyone's sake."

"How can you?"

"By doing what I've always done. Showing myself in the village. Making myself of use. It's harder to gossip about someone who does you a kindness."

"Harder," Winnifred said grimly, "but not impossible."

Chapter Three

*M*ark rarely used the gig when paying calls on his parishioners in the village, and never in the summer. He enjoyed the walk back to the vicarage too much to forego it. The gently curving path ran beneath a canopy of trees alongside the harebell-blanketed banks of the Worthy River.

Though one couldn't exactly call it a river.

It was merely a tributary of the River Brue, and a smallish one at that. But it was one of the loveliest places in Shepton Worthy. Soft with color and fragrance, and kissed by sweet summer breezes.

As he walked, his coat thrown over one arm, and his cravat loosened in a minor concession to the heat, Mark turned his face up to the clear blue sky, letting the sun warm his skin.

A muffled sound came from up ahead. He recognized it immediately. It was a sound he often heard when ministering to the sick and ill, or when sitting with the recently bereaved. It was someone weeping softly.

A *lady* weeping.

He slowed his step, debating whether or not to proceed. Avoidance was the easiest course. It would save him the trouble of interfering, and very likely spare the embarrassment of the poor woman. She obviously didn't want to be disturbed. Why else had she come to such a remote spot to do her weeping?

But he couldn't walk away. The villagers were his responsibility. If he could give someone comfort or counsel, he was duty bound to do it.

Advancing carefully through the trees, he passed under a low-hanging branch and through a gap in a wild tangle of shrubbery. No sooner had he done so that he came to a jarring halt. His breath stopped in his chest.

It was Beryl Burnham.

Garbed in a full-skirted white cotton day dress, she was sitting near the river, her arms folded over her updrawn knees, and her forehead resting on her forearms. Her shoulders shook with the strength of her quiet sobs.

His heart clenched hard.

He hadn't seen her since church on Sunday, nearly three days ago. He was beginning to suspect she was avoiding him. An uneasy thought. She'd have only one reason to do so. A reason that, when contemplated, made Mark's neck grow hot beneath his collar in a mortified blush.

Had Henry said something?

Mark doubted it. And yet…Beryl hadn't sought him out. Hadn't offered to call on sick parishioners with him, or to assist with preparations for the summer fete. Even in church, she'd studiously evaded his gaze.

Mark had noticed her particularly, just as he always did, his eyes gravitating to her against his will. She'd been seated near the front—along with her mother, sister, and aunt—in the row behind the pew reserved for the Rivenhall family. Nothing had seemed to be wrong with her then. She'd sat and stood in time with the rest of the congregation, had sung the hymns and recited the prayers. And yet he hadn't been able to rid himself of the feeling that something was wrong.

And something *was* wrong, if her tears were any indication.

For an instant, he felt an overwhelming sense of powerlessness. What in the world could he do to help her? This person for whom he cared so very much? It was gone as quickly as it came. His own feelings for her didn't matter. He was a curate, and she was a member of his church. He knew what must be done.

Emerging from the woods, he crossed the grass and sank down on the riverbank at her side, dropping his hat, coat, and the books he'd been carrying down next to him in a disorganized heap.

She lifted her head with a start. Her blue-green eyes were swollen. "Mark." She hastily wiped at her cheeks. "What are you doing here?"

"I often come this way when I walk home." He withdrew his white linen handkerchief from his waistcoat pocket and offered it to her. It was clean and freshly pressed, courtesy of Mrs. Phillips, the kindly housekeeper at the vicarage.

Beryl took it without looking at him and used it to dry her tears. Her slender fingers were trembling. "I believed I had privacy. I wouldn't have come here otherwise."

"Forgive the intrusion. I saw you through the trees, and…I thought you might need a friend." He let the silence between them lengthen, waiting as she finished blotting her eyes. The delicate scent of her teased at his senses. Sunshine and elder-flower. It was wild and honey sweet, and so achingly familiar that it made his heart hurt. "What's wrong?"

"Nothing."

"It doesn't look like nothing. It looks like something has upset you very much. I'd like to help if I can."

She looked away from him to stare out at the river. Her hair was falling loose from the simple chignon she wore at her nape. Wispy golden strands clung to her damp face.

"You can talk to me," he said. "You do know that, don't you?"

Fresh tears pooled in her eyes. "What is there to say? You already know everything."

A jolt of apprehension narrowed his gaze. "Everything about what?"

"About why I left Shepton Worthy last year." A stray tear rolled down her cheek, glittering in the sunlight. She dashed it away. "And you needn't pretend ignorance. My mother already admitted that she told Mr. Venable. I can only assume he relayed it all to you the first chance he got."

"You assume wrong."

She cast him an uncertain glance. "What has he told you, then? If not the whole of it—"

"None of it. Nothing about you." Mark hadn't been taken into the antiquated vicar's confidence in ages. It was nothing personal. Venable was simply too busy nursing his own physical ailments to give any thought to the health of his congregation. "I thought... That is, everyone understood that your aunt insisted you accompany her. That there was no way you could refuse without causing a rift in the family."

"*Everyone* understood? Not everyone, surely."

Mark inwardly winced. There *had* been gossip. Cruel whispers about Beryl having gone away to have a child. No one had dared repeat such rumors to his face, but hearing them secondhand had been bad enough. He'd been outraged, of course. Outraged and…bemused.

Beryl and Jack?

The very idea was too ludicrous to consider. Jack hadn't set foot in England in years. Which made it a ridiculous rumor, as well as a malicious one. Anyone with half a brain in their head would know there was no substance to it.

"You know how villages can be," Mark said.

"Yes. I'd expected there would be talk. But that it should be so sordid…" Her voice cracked. "And it's all my fault. If only I'd been…"

"What?"

"Braver. Stronger. I don't know." She rested her forehead back on her arms, inhaling a shallow, shuddering breath. "I'm so unhappy, Mark."

His heart twisted. "Is it because of your engagement to Henry?"

She shook her head. "It's not because of Henry."

Mark felt the faintest flicker of disappointment. Felt it and was ashamed of it. Such feelings did him no credit. They were unbrotherly. Unchristian, even. He was done with all of that. He'd had an entire year to get over her. A year to accept that she was marrying his brother. That she was nothing to him but a friend.

But it wasn't nothing, their friendship. It never had been. Not to him.

"I was unhappy long before I became engaged to Henry," she said. "Long before we ever moved to Shepton Worthy."

Mark found that hard to believe. From the moment he'd met Beryl, nearly ten years ago when her family had first come to the Grange, he'd been impressed by her quiet good nature. Her kindness and unruffled serenity. She'd never been boisterous or silly. Not vain or mean-spirited. Indeed, he supposed she *was* rather self-contained at times. Prone to retreating into herself.

As a younger man, he'd made a mystery of her. But as he'd grown older, he'd come to recognize her as an incredibly thoughtful person. A young lady readily willing to sacrifice her own comfort for that of her friends and family, and for those in circumstances not so enviable as her own.

Was it possible that, all this time, her quiet nature had been a mask for some manner of private unhappiness?

He hated to think so.

"You've never seemed unhappy," he said. "Not so long as I've known you."

"Because I'm a fraud. Because m-my whole life is a lie." Her voice broke on a stifled sob.

He instinctively lifted a hand to touch her, only to draw it back, too uncertain of himself to offer her comfort.

Dash it all!

This wasn't about him. It had nothing to do with his own feelings, and everything to do with hers.

He set his hand gently on the curve of her spine, just between her shoulder blades. The heat of her skin, toasted from the sun, warmed his palm and fingers. He felt it all the way through the fabric of her fitted cotton bodice. It stirred a wealth of unspoken emotion in him. Made his voice hoarse, and his pulse stutter. "You're not a fraud. You're the kindest person I know."

The kindest. The dearest.

"I want to help you if I can," he said. "If you'll permit me."

Tears clogged Beryl's throat. She was thankful for the sheltering trees and overgrown shrubbery that ran wild along this side of the river. It was bad enough that Mark should see her in such a distressed condition. She couldn't imagine how she'd manage facing anyone else. "You can't help me," she said. "You don't even know me. Not really. No one does."

Mark's hand was a warm, reassuring weight on her back. "Then tell me. Tell me what's happened to make you so unhappy."

She squeezed her eyes shut against another onslaught of tears, and she wished—oh, how she wished—that there was a reason. That she could pin her sorrow onto a specific incident.

But no such incident existed.

Indeed, the day had started pleasantly enough. She'd accompanied Winnifred to Rivenhall Park to see that horse she was so enamored of. They'd stopped in to visit Henry, of course. He'd seemed a trifle irritated to have his work interrupted without notice. Irritated, but still unfailingly polite. Afterward, he'd escorted them back to the Grange in his carriage.

The rest of the day had been taken up with visits from acquaintances in the village, and with helping Mama with plans for the wedding. It was a joyful time—or should have been. Beryl was certain that any other lady would have found it so.

But she hadn't. She'd been too much in her own head to take pleasure in anything. Too weighted down with an inexplicable sorrow.

"Nothing," she said. "I'm just…I'm an unhappy person."

Mark made a scoffing noise.

"It's true. Ever since I was a girl. I can remember the exact moment I realized it." She wiped her face again with his handkerchief. "I was thirteen. And one day it was suddenly there."

"What was?"

"This sadness inside of me. *Here*. Like a leaden weight." She pressed her fingertips to her breastbone. That aching place, just above the line of her corset busk. "I told my mother, and she asked me what I had to be sad about. And there was no reason. No cause. I only knew how it felt. Like I was alone, and no one loved me."

Mark leaned closer, his posture protective. "You're not alone." His voice deepened. "And you *are* loved. Deeply loved."

"I know that. I knew it then. But that's the closest thing to what it feels like." She bent her head back to her knees. "It's been with me ever since. This weight. It's why I had to leave last year."

He hesitated for the space of a heartbeat. She could almost hear the wheels in his mind, swiftly processing the various implications of her words—none of them to the good. "What do you mean? Why did you have to leave?"

She was silent for a long moment.

He slid his hand over the curve of her spine. Gently, gently. "Beryl?"

She swallowed hard. "I've grown accustomed to taking a sachet of sleeping powder at night. It helps me to sleep when the sadness is at its worst. Two weeks before I left for Paris

43

with Aunt Hortensia, I took several of them at the same time. The next morning, Mama was unable to wake me."

Mark's hand stilled on her back. Tension vibrated in his touch. "You weren't trying to—"

"No. I didn't want to die. I just wanted it all to stop. I wanted *this* to stop." Her fingers dug into her breastbone. "I needed a reprieve from it, if only for one night. And the sleeping powder wasn't strong enough in a single dose. I didn't realize—"

"My God, Beryl."

"I know. I *know*."

"How did you—"

"Mama sent for Mr. Cooper, who managed to revive me. He told Mama—" She broke off. What Mr. Cooper had advised didn't bear repeating. The vile man was gone now. She'd never have to see him again. "It doesn't matter what. In the end, Aunt Hortensia decided it would be best if I went away awhile for a rest. For my nerves. Because I'd fallen quite to pieces. Not because I was with child or—"

"I never believed that," Mark said fiercely. "Not for a single second. I knew that something was amiss, but I thought—"

"That I merely needed cheering up?" She offered him a weak smile. "Hence your amusing letters."

He grimaced. "I was oversimplifying things, clearly."

"They did help. I looked forward to them so much. Now I'm home, I don't know what I shall do without them."

His hand moved on her back. "I suppose I must resort to rallying your spirits in person."

"I'm afraid they're beyond rallying." She regretted the words as soon as she uttered them. Regretted them, and hated herself for thinking—for feeling—as she did. In her worst moments, she was no better than the despicable creature described in the *Provincial Medical and Surgical Gazette.* "Forgive me. I must sound like the worst sort of self-pitying—"

"Not at all. I'd rather you were honest with me, than hiding your true feelings behind some sort of mask. You don't need one with me. I hope you know that."

"Oh, Mark. I don't want to lay a burden on you."

"Please do. It's what I'm here for, to help shoulder the burdens of others. It would be my privilege to shoulder yours. I don't like to see anyone in pain, you least of all."

"I'm not any more important than anyone else."

"You are to me."

Her heart gave a queer double thump. She didn't know why. This was Mark she was talking to. Her friend. Her soon-to-be brother-in-law.

"Tell me something," he said. "This weight of sadness, is it truly always with you?"

She looked out over the water. It flowed steadily over the ridges in the riverbed and the low outcroppings of stone, rippling in gentle harmony with the summer breeze that rustled the leaves. "Not always. Sometimes it's overshadowed by happier moments. But there never seem to be enough of those. Not lately."

Mark graciously refrained from mentioning her upcoming wedding to his brother. "And you can tie it to no cause?"

"I've had it too long to believe it connected to anything. It's a part of me. Something to be endured. There's no getting rid of it."

He paused, seeming to consider. "Have you tried—"

"I'm dreadfully fond of you, Mark, but if you ask me whether or not I've prayed over it, I'm going to pitch you straight into the Worthy."

Mark's mouth hitched. "I wasn't going to ask anything of the sort."

"Good. Because I *have* prayed. It hasn't done me any good at all. I expect God has more important matters to concern himself with than my trifling problems."

"You *are* important. And faith does help. But we can't abdicate our own responsibilities. If there's action to be taken, we must take it, both for ourselves, and for each other."

Action? What action was left, other than to follow Mr. Cooper's gruesome recommendations.

She would die, rather.

"Do you think I haven't?" she asked. "That I haven't tried everything I can to—"

"Easy," he murmured. "I know you, despite what you think. I know you'll have fought like a tiger to rid yourself of this feeling. Trust that much, at least."

His strong fingers brushed the bare nape of her neck. Soft. Tender. It was almost a caress. Enough to send a delicate shiver down Beryl's spine.

Mark must have felt it, too, for he quickly removed his hand. It seemed as though he might have said something more, but in that same instant, a gentle gust of wind caught his tall hat from the pile at his side. It tumbled down over the grassy slope of the riverbank, coming to a halt on a cluster of flowering weeds. He made no effort to chase it.

She looked up at him in question.

His expression turned wry. "'There are few moments in a man's existence when he experiences so much ludicrous distress as when he is in pursuit of his own hat.'"

A slow smile spread over her face. "*The Pickwick Club*," she said, temporarily diverted. "I'm amazed you can recite it so readily."

"But not faithfully."

"Still," she said. "It must have been more than six years since we read it together."

Along with books on every other imaginable subject, the library at Rivenhall Park contained most of Mr. Dickens's works. One summer, soon after Mark had come home from university, the two of them had torn through them all, sharing the stories between them, and trading quotes like secrets. Mark had always preferred the humorous passages. He'd seemed to relish coaxing a smile from her.

"I'd like to claim superior memory. The truth is"—he lifted a book from the stack beside him—"I've been reading it aloud to one of my ill parishioners."

She sat up straighter. "Is that the same copy?"

"It is. Look here." He opened the leather-and-cloth cover. In the top right-hand corner of the engraved frontispiece, a tiny butterfly was sketched in long-faded black ink.

She touched it with her fingertip. Memory flooded through her. Long days spent immersed in a fictional world. The excitement she'd felt, looking forward to the next scene and the next. Excitement she and Mark had shared together. "I don't know what possessed me to draw in it. Your brother would be appalled."

"Henry doesn't read novels. Besides," Mark said, "I asked you to do it."

"Did you?" She didn't recall it. All she could remember was the illicit thrill of dipping a sharpened quill into the inkpot and sketching the tiny body, antennae, and wings. It had felt like a crime. "I suppose you must have done. I wouldn't have dared otherwise."

"I wanted something to remember you by," he said. "That summer was one of the best times of my life."

A pang of nostalgia pricked at her soul, already so raw and aching. "Mine as well."

His gaze was upon her. She felt the weight of it just as she'd felt the weight of his touch. "Would you like me to read to you?"

Her heart leapt. *Yes*, she wanted to say. *Please*. But she wasn't the girl she'd been at eighteen. Maturity had made her cautious. "Here?"

"It's quite private."

It was at that. The trees curved down around the riverbank, shrouding their lonely patch of harebell-covered grass from view. It was cool and secluded—half light, half shadow—and so quiet that she could almost convince herself that she and Mark were the only two people on earth.

"Very well," she said.

He turned the gilt-edged pages. "I'll start at the beginning of the passage about Mr. Pickwick's hat, shall I?" When she made no objection, he began to read, his deep voice clear and steady. "'Man is but mortal; and there is a point beyond which human courage cannot extend...'"

Beryl lay back on the grass, staring up at the blue sky that peeked through the branches of the trees. She was weary from weeping, but as Mark read, she felt a sense of increasing peace. She could rest here. She might even fall asleep. And he'd be here to watch over her. To keep her safe from harm.

It was a foolish notion. There was no need to be kept safe. She wasn't in any danger. The only peril she faced was from herself—from her own unruly emotions. What could Mark do about those? Nothing at all. She knew that. And yet...

Some of the tension eased from her limbs. She draped one arm across her midsection, letting her eyes drift shut as she listened to him.

A long while passed before Mark stopped reading.

"Have I bored you to sleep?" he asked.

She opened her eyes to find him leaning over her, blocking the sunlight from her face. She smiled. "Indeed not. I was only thinking."

"About what?"

"That it's been ages since I've heard you read anything but a sermon."

"Is that all." He drew back as she sat up and dusted the grass from her gown. "If you'd like me to read to you again, you need only say so. I hope you know that I'm yours to command."

Her pulse gave an odd flutter. "As if I would presume to command you."

"You know what I mean. If it would lift your spirits—"

"Being with you always lifts my spirits. But it's rather more complicated than that." She smoothed her skirts over her updrawn knees. "You mustn't feel obliged to try to cheer me just because I've confided in you."

"It's not obligation. It's—" He stopped. "What I mean to say is…" He fell quiet a moment. "This burden of yours—this sadness—I want you to leave it with me for a day or two."

Her chest constricted. She was grateful for his kindness. It was well meant, however wrong-headed. "It's not something I can hand off at will. And even if I could…" Her eyes met his. "You can't fix this, Mark. You can't fix *me*."

He gave her a brief, lopsided smile. "Of course not," he said. "You're not broken."

Chapter Four

*C*losing his well-worn copy of *The Posthumous Papers of the Pickwick Club*, Mark rose from the shabby chintz armchair angled beside Mrs. Arbuthnot's sickbed. The movement triggered another storm of barking from the little black dog curled at her feet. He was a dubious-looking canine of no particular pedigree—though his bulging eyes, wiry hair, and plumed tail identified him as some unholy mixture of pug, terrier, and spaniel.

"Don't mind him, Mr. Rivenhall." Mrs. Arbuthnot's speech was slightly slurred. "He fancies he's protecting me."

Mark smiled. "I don't mind. Ernest and I are old friends."

Ernest responded to that statement by curling his lip to bare his snaggled teeth.

Mrs. Arbuthnot summoned the little dog to her with an age-spotted hand. "I would that you were. My daughter's husband won't tolerate dogs in the house. If I can't find a place for Ernest before she comes to fetch me, he'll have to be destroyed. Mrs. Doolittle's offered to do the job with chloroform."

Mark's smile evaporated. Ernest was no prize, but he was a young dog yet, and a loyal one. He deserved better. "Is there no one who can take him for you?"

"No, sir. Mrs. White down the lane was considering it, but she's a fastidious sort, and don't like any creatures leaving a mess."

Mrs. Arbuthnot's own cottage wasn't messy any more. Most of the furnishings had been sold, and what was left of her belongings were in the process of being packed into a large trunk. A severe episode of apoplexy earlier in the year had left her paralyzed on one side. She was no longer capable of living independently.

It was Mark who had contacted her daughter and made arrangements for Mrs. Arbuthnot to go and live with her. At the time, he'd assumed Ernest would be welcome.

"She'll be here next week," Mrs. Arbuthnot said.

Mark took her good hand in his and gave it a gentle squeeze. "Let me see what I can do."

A brisk knock at the door announced the arrival of Dr. Black. He came into the cottage with the ease of one who visited daily, and had no need to await an invitation to enter. "Mrs. Arbuthnot. Mr. Rivenhall." He removed his hat. "Good morning."

Simon Black was a tall, rangy young man, with a mop of fair hair, and side-whiskers trimmed short on either side of his narrow face. His hazel eyes were sharp, his expression as intelligent as it was compassionate. In short, he was nothing at all like Mr. Cooper, the rough surgeon who had preceded him.

Mark often encountered Dr. Black in the course of performing his parish duties. He'd come to value the man's judgment and discretion, and to look on him as something like a friend. After exchanging greetings with him, Mark took his leave of Mrs. Arbuthnot. He lingered outside in the lane until the young doctor emerged.

Black regarded him with upraised brows.

"I hoped to have a word with you," Mark said.

"I've got another patient to stop in on. You can accompany me part of the way if you like."

Mark fell in beside him, the two of them walking in the direction of the river. He didn't say anything. Not at first. The subject was too important to treat lightly.

Black shot a look at the book in Mark's hand. "Dickens?" His lips twitched. "Not the Bible?"

"Not today, no." Or any other day this week. Mrs. Arbuthnot wasn't at death's door. She needed cheering. Dickens always did the trick. If not him, it would be romantic poetry. Shakespeare, Wordsworth, or Keats. And Mark was in no mood to be reciting love poems.

"If only I'd known that literary works were an alternative text." Black smiled wryly. "My career might have taken a different path."

"You considered the church?"

"Not I. My father. It's the fate of most third sons, I believe. Whether they be spiritually inclined or not."

Mark gave him a distracted glance. Simon Black was well educated and spoke in the tones of a gentleman, but up to now, he hadn't been very forthcoming about his forbears. Mark hadn't liked to press him. One never knew if there was a tragedy lurking in someone's past. "Your father was a member of the gentry?"

"Something like that." Black's expression sobered. "He's the Earl of Harbury."

"Ah." Mark recognized the name. The earl was a staunch conservative, as well as being one of the wealthiest men in the southwest of England. "He doesn't approve of your chosen career?"

"It isn't the medical profession he objects to. It's my liberal views he deplores. That, and my preference for working with the poor. We're not estranged, but…I've done my best to limit our connection. It's why I prefer the relationship not to become common knowledge."

"Understandable." Mark stared straight ahead as they walked. It was another warm summer day in Shepton Worthy, everything bright and blooming with fragrance. He was too preoccupied to appreciate it.

"Mrs. Arbuthnot's doing better, you know," Black said. "If that's what it is that's troubling you."

"I'm glad to hear it. But that isn't what I wanted to speak with you about. It's something else. A general question."

"Go on."

"What do you know about melancholy?"

"Specifically?"

"How to treat it." Mark paused. "How to cure it."

"There is no cure," Black said. "Not as far as I'm concerned."

Mark's spirits sank. He'd suspected as much. Still, to hear it from a medical man was akin to a death knell.

"Of course," Black continued, "there are plenty who would tell you the opposite. Have a look inside any apothecary's shop and you'll see shelves of patent medicines infused with opiates and stimulants. Not a one of them is a cure, only a means to sleep longer, or to stay awake for days at a time, depending on the tonic one takes. Many of my patients swear by them."

"You don't believe they work?"

Black shook his head. "It's quackery."

"Are there no legitimate treatments for melancholy? The genuine affliction?"

"As to that…" Black adjusted his battered leather medical bag in his hand. "Many practitioners prefer the more extreme methods. Ice baths. Various deprivations. Even electrical shocks with one of those newfangled electricity machines." His brow creased. "I suppose that's the basis of all of it—to shock the patient out of the melancholy by some dramatic means."

"You don't think it's possible?"

"Not without damaging the patient's body—or his spirit. There are better methods of treatment to my mind, but as I said, there's no cure. Not for the acute variety."

Mark ran his hand over the back of his neck. He didn't like the sound of any of it. "*Are* there many varieties?"

"Naturally. It sometimes arises from a particular situation. The birth of a child. A death in the family. Guilt over some kind of misconduct. Those episodes generally resolve themselves at some point."

That much Mark knew. Over the years, he'd encountered similar evidence of melancholy among those of his parishioners who were undergoing various trials of life. He'd talked with them. Prayed with them. "And the other kind? This acute variety that you mention?"

"It has no discernable cause."

"And therefore, no treatment?"

Black flashed him an interested look. "Are we discussing someone in particular?"

Mark didn't reply. He wasn't about to divulge Beryl's secrets, not to the village doctor or anyone.

"Well, in general terms then…" Black squinted into the distance. "I'd say that, though there's no cure for that kind of melancholy, one can certainly learn to manage it."

"What do you recommend?"

"Physical occupation. Add to that, plenty of sunshine, good food, and a good night's sleep. The latter can be aided with hydrate of chloral, but other than that, I'm reluctant to prescribe medications."

"Physical occupation," Mark repeated. Beryl had been engaged in such for as long as he'd known her. If she wasn't paying calls on the sick and needy—reading to them, tidying their cottages, and doing their shopping—she was volunteering for various ladies' committees. She'd never been idle. Only restless, she'd said. Restless and, apparently, plagued by melancholy.

Mark had never noticed. He'd only seen what he wanted to see. Her goodness. Her willingness to be of service. She'd never shown him what lurked beneath. And he'd never troubled himself to look very hard.

He felt a keen sense of having let her down.

"Keeping oneself busy, in other words," Black went on. "I've found it's often easier for male patients than for females. Ladies are sedentary creatures by nature." He looked down the lane, his attention caught by two riders approaching. His lips compressed. "Most ladies, that is."

Mark followed his gaze. It was Winnifred Burnham. Garbed in a dark blue habit, she was riding sidesaddle on an enormous dapple-gray stallion. A harried groom rode a full length behind her. Mark recognized the fellow from the stables at Rivenhall Park.

He frowned. It had been his understanding that, when riding Henry's stallion, Winnifred kept to the grounds of the Park. When had she begun venturing farther?

She slowed as she approached. The gilt buttons that ornamented her form-fitting bodice flashed in the sun. "Mr. Rivenhall. Dr. Black."

"Miss Winnifred," Mark said. "Good day to you."

Though Winnifred inclined her head in acknowledgment, she was looking at Black, not Mark. Her eyes narrowed. "Do you have something you wish to say to me, sir?"

Black returned her gaze. He seemed to be standing a little taller. "Such as?"

"Another piece of well-meant advice? Another censure?"

"I wouldn't dream of it, ma'am."

"Oh, wouldn't you." Winnifred glared at him a moment longer and then trotted on. "Good day, gentlemen."

When she'd passed, Black's shoulders visibly relaxed. "Infernal female," he muttered. "All I ever said to her was that she'd best be careful cantering down the road on that beast, lest she hurt herself—or someone else. You'd think I'd insulted the girl."

"To Miss Winnifred that *would* be an insult. She's the most accomplished horsewoman in Shepton Worthy."

"She's a pain in my backside is what she is. But I'll say no more on the subject, seeing as how you're on the verge of being connected with the family. Once Sir Henry marries Miss Burnham—" Black looked at Mark. "I say, she's not very like her sister, is she?"

"You haven't met her yet?"

Black shook his head. "I haven't had the pleasure."

"No," Mark said. "Miss Burnham is nothing like her sister. She's…"

She was different.

Not only quieter and more thoughtful, she was—at least to Mark's mind—the more beautiful of the Burnham sisters. Where Winnifred's blondness was delicate and pale as silver, Beryl's was as golden as summer sunlight. It warmed him just to think of her.

The way her dark, winged brows arched over her blue-green eyes. The way her left cheek dimpled when her mouth curved in a genuine smile.

How long had it been since he'd seen that dimple?

Too long.

Black laughed. "She defies description, I see."

Heat rose under Mark's collar. "Miss Burnham is all that's good in the world, is what I was going to say."

A grin remained on Black's face, but in his eyes shone an all-too-knowing glint of sympathy. "If that's the case, then I must congratulate your brother on his good fortune."

"Yes." Mark somehow managed a smile of his own. It was as false as his words were true. "My brother is a fortunate man."

Beryl entered the church to find it teeming with industry. The ladies on the committee to oversee this year's summer fete were gathered near the front, heaps of flowers, ribbon, and greenery strewn about them on the pews and the floor.

Smoothing the skirts of her blue grenadine afternoon dress, Beryl slowly approached. It had taken all of her courage to come today, knowing what the gossip had been.

But it wasn't only the gossip that had given her pause.

It was the prospect of encountering Mark again. She hadn't seen him since that dreadful day on the riverbank. He'd been compassionate then, just as he always was, but she hadn't any doubt that, when given time to reflect on the matter, his opinion of her would have altered.

How could it not? She'd told him everything. Had wept and felt sorry for herself and made herself ridiculous.

Leave this burden with me for a day or two, he'd said.

That had been nearly two full days ago. She hadn't seen him since.

Granted, the preparations for the summer fete were in full swing. And Mr. Venable was ill, as were several other people in the village. Mark had more than enough to occupy his time without troubling himself over Beryl's problems.

And really, she hadn't expected him to solve anything for her. She knew there was no solution. What she wanted—needed—was his friendship. And after that day on the riverbank…

She very much feared she may have lost it.

"Miss Burnham!" Having caught sight of Beryl, several of the ladies called out in greeting.

Mrs. Doolittle was among them, her eyes as shrewdly assessing as ever. "Have you come to offer your assistance?"

"I have," Beryl said. "I hope I'm not too late?"

"Your timing is impeccable." Mrs. White, another elderly village lady, stood next to Mrs. Doolittle. Her smile of greeting was a bit warmer, her plump face aglow. "I was only this moment mentioning your name to Mrs. Malvern. We feared you wouldn't have the time to assist us, what with your wedding to plan. Which is a great pity, for we could very much use your knees."

Beryl gave her a bewildered look. "My *knees*?"

"Yes, indeed," Mrs. Malvern said. Wife of the village draper, she presented a fashionable picture in her matching skirt and paletot of rose-colored percale. "Mr. Rivenhall has given us permission to decorate inside the church this year. We've just been determining who among us is best suited to adorn the ends of the pews with flowers and greenery."

"One must kneel down," Mrs. White added in a hushed tone. "So difficult on the knees, you know, when one is a lady of a certain age."

Mrs. Doolittle nodded in brisk agreement. "Youth is required for such tasks."

"I'd be glad to do it," Beryl said. "And any other tasks you haven't yet assigned." She addressed the rest of the ladies as a whole. "I apologize it's taken me so many days to make an appearance."

"We've managed well enough so far." Mrs. Malvern briefly clasped Beryl's hand. "But it is good to have you back, Miss Burnham. And not only for selfish reasons. Though I do hope you'll still be contributing your whitework to sell at the fete?"

"Oh yes." Beryl brightened. "I've embroidered ever so many handkerchiefs, several sets of linens, and a half dozen little baby smocks made of the softest muslin I could find." She'd been working on them all year, stitching tiny images of flowers, honeybees, and dragonflies onto the edges of the fabric in delicate motifs.

"Splendid," Mrs. Malvern said. "Though I don't know how you found the time. If I was ever so fortunate as to go to Paris, they'd have to drag me away from the shops." She tipped her head closer, sinking her voice. "Speaking of which, I can't wait to learn more about these Parisian gowns of yours. Is it true that Mr. Worth designed your wedding dress?"

"He did, ma'am. It hasn't yet arrived, but I expect it to be delivered soon."

"When it does, you must bring it to the Emporium. My husband is anxious to have a look at it. That is, if it wouldn't be too much of an imposition."

"No, indeed," Beryl said. "I'd be glad to show it to him."

"A costly thing, a Parisian gown," Mrs. Doolittle remarked.

Beryl pasted on a smile. "My aunt has been exceedingly generous. I'm very grateful to her."

"So you should be," Mrs. White said. "A whole year in Paris. Such an adventure!"

"Oh yes." Mrs. Doolittle exchanged a speaking glance with one of the other ladies on the committee. "*Quite* an adventure."

There was an eruption of tittering laughter.

Mrs. Malvern responded to it with a stern look. "Do try to remember to keep your voices down, ladies. Mr. Rivenhall is working on his Sunday sermon."

Beryl affected not to notice the laughter and the whispered words. At this stage, confronting the perpetrators would do nothing to quell the gossip. Chances were it would only enflame it. Better to keep herself to herself. To be placid and kind—and completely uninteresting. Boredom was death to gossip. Given time, it would strangle for lack of oxygen.

She glanced at the open door at the back of the church. "Is he in his office?"

"He is," Mrs. Malvern said. "Do you need to speak with him?"

Beryl bit her lip. She did want to speak with him, but not if it meant disturbing his work.

Mrs. Malvern seemed to read her mind. "You needn't worry about interrupting him, dear. He usually breaks for a cup of tea roundabout this time." She gave Beryl an encouraging smile. "Go ahead. The decorations will still be here when you return."

With a murmured word of thanks, Beryl made her way through the open door and down a short hallway. At the end, the door to Mark's office stood open, his frock coat and hat hanging on the back of it. Mark was inside, seated behind his cluttered desk, scratching over a paper with a sharpened quill.

Beryl froze in the doorway. She couldn't help but stare. She'd never seen Mark in such a state of undress. Not only was his waistcoat unbuttoned, the sleeves of his linen shirt were rolled up, exposing a bare expanse of leanly muscled forearm. The sight of it made her feel rather strange. As if butterflies were unfurling their wings in her stomach, preparing to take flight.

A foolish thought. And an equally foolish feeling. She was only a little nervous, that was all. Who wouldn't be after what had happened the last time they met?

Moistening her lips, she rapped lightly on the doorframe.

Mark glanced up from writing his sermon. His blue eyes widened. "Beryl!" He rose from his chair so quickly that he bumped his desk, unsettling a pot of ink. He righted it at once, but not before a quantity of black ink spilled out.

She rushed forward to help him move his papers out of the way. "Mind your sermon."

"It's fine. No harm done."

"Thank goodness. Have you a handkerchief?"

Producing one from the pocket of his trousers, he reached to blot the spilled ink at the same moment Beryl reached to take the handkerchief from his hand. They brushed against each other, nearly unsettling the inkpot once more.

She rested a hand on Mark's chest with a huff of laughter. "This isn't efficient at all."

He stared down at her. "No. It isn't."

Her smile faded as she returned his gaze. Something seemed to pass between them. She didn't know what it was. But it made warmth pool low in her belly. "Mark, I—"

"You'd better move away," he said. "You'll stain your dress."

Her eyes dropped to her skirts. Standing wide over petticoats and crinoline, they were pressed, rather intimately, against Mark's legs, nowhere near the ink spill. She nevertheless turned and went to the opposite side of his desk. "I'm sorry to have disturbed your work. Mrs. Malvern said you'd be breaking for tea."

"I lost track of time." He wiped his hands on his handkerchief before disposing of it. "But you haven't disturbed me. I'm glad to see you."

"Are you?" She hated how hopeful she sounded.

"I'm always glad to see you." He motioned for her to sit down. "Please."

She reluctantly took a seat. Her heart was still beating swiftly. A result of that unsettling encounter behind his desk. Goodness, the way he'd looked at her! The warmth in his blue gaze had practically been a smolder. She'd never known Mark Rivenhall could look that way. Not at her, or anyone.

But he wasn't smoldering now. Far worse. Once again seated behind his desk, he was regarding her with a look of concern.

"How are you?" he asked. "How are you feeling?"

Folding her hands in her lap, Beryl recalled herself to the reason she'd come. "Mortified," she said frankly.

The concern in his eyes deepened. He leaned forward in his chair. "About what?"

"Sharing all of those things with you. Those private things. I shouldn't have done so." Her words tumbled over each other in a rush. She made an effort to bring her speech back to normal. "I hope that you'll forget we ever spoke on the subject."

Understanding registered on his face. "You regret talking to me about it."

"Very much. I don't know why I went on as I did. It was badly done of me. Afterward, I know you must have been shocked at my behavior."

He continued to look at her, frowning slightly. A studying look, as if he was keen to read her. To learn her. "You did nothing wrong."

She tugged at the finger of her glove. A small, agitated movement. She had to remind herself to be still.

"I was honored that you confided in me," he said. "My only regret is that I didn't know of your burden sooner."

"How could you?"

"By listening to you. By paying proper attention. I thought…" He stopped himself. "It doesn't matter what I thought. The fact is, I feel as though I've failed you. But I mean to make it right. To be here for you as much as I'm able, even if all I can do is listen."

"That's very generous of you, but—"

"You must want someone to talk to on occasion," he said. "Someone to whom you can speak plainly."

Beryl felt a stab of yearning. How lovely it would be to have someone to confide in. Someone like Mark Rivenhall. And yet...

She couldn't imagine ever doing so again. Having done so once was quite enough. It had been selfish and self-indulgent. Not at all the type of thing she should be making a habit of.

"You're mistaken," she said. "I don't usually indulge myself in that way."

"Perhaps you should. If not to me, then..." He paused for several seconds, seeming to come to a decision. "Have you considered talking to Henry?"

Her mouth nearly fell open. "You haven't told him?"

"No, no. I would never violate your confidence. But the two of you are soon to be married. You might consider—"

"No." She was adamant. "I don't want Henry to know. He'd think—" That she was being stupid and ungrateful, that's what he'd think. That she was indulging a desire for feminine dramatics, something for which he had no patience at all.

But she couldn't say such things. Not to Henry's brother of all people.

"Henry wouldn't understand," she said instead.

"Probably not." Mark's brow furrowed. "You don't feel you can talk to your mother? Or to your sister?"

She'd tried to talk to her mother. Had been compelled to on occasion, even against her will. After the incident with the sleeping powder, there hadn't been any choice. But though she loved Beryl absolutely, Mama couldn't tolerate defects. It was the same as with her roses. She required them to be beautiful, pleasing, and perfect. Anything less was quickly cut away and disposed of. Out of sight and out of mind.

As for Winnifred, she was too young to understand. Too caught up in her own affairs. She wasn't even aware of the true reason Beryl had gone away last year. No one had wanted to burden her with the details. The most she knew was that Beryl had been blue-deviled, and that Aunt Hortensia had suggested a pleasure trip to boost her spirits.

Blue-deviled. As if it were a condition of brief duration, and not an affliction that had plagued Beryl for most of her life.

"There's no one. You're the first person I've ever said any of those things to." She exhaled. "I wish I hadn't said them."

His expression softened. "I'm glad you did. And I hope you'll see fit to confide in me again. But I understand if you'd rather not share your feelings with anyone." He gave her a fleeting smile. "I had an idea about that, actually." Opening the drawer of his desk, he withdrew a small book bound in dark green cloth. "I bought this for you at Malvern's Emporium."

"For me?" She took it from his outstretched hand. "Thank you, but—"

"I was going to stop by the Grange this evening and give it to you."

She opened the book, expecting she knew not what. But it was no novel. No book of poetry. Quite the reverse. The pages were all blank. Her gaze lifted to Mark's in question.

"It's a journal," he said. "A place for you to record your thoughts and feelings."

"Like a young lady's diary?" She flipped slowly through the empty pages.

"You don't approve? Many ladies keep a journal, I believe. Even Her Majesty."

"So did Winnie when she was a girl. It seemed rather silly."

"It can be as serious or silly as you wish. The point is, it's yours. A repository for your sadness, on those days it becomes too much to bear. You can put it there, in those pages." He paused. "That was my idea anyway."

Her throat constricted. She had the sudden fear that she might cry.

"If it doesn't appeal to you," he said, "you're quite free to discard it."

Her gloved fingers tightened on the journal. "Indeed, I won't." She lifted her gaze back to his. "Thank you, Mark. How very thoughtful you are."

He smiled at her then. One of his warm smiles. The kind he used to give her before she left Shepton Worthy. The kind that said he was her friend. That he'd *always* be her friend. "Mind you," he said, "it's not my only idea. I've several others I'm working out."

And then Beryl feared she really would cry if she didn't take her leave.

"I shall look forward to them." She stood. "Forgive me, I've taken enough of your time. The ladies are waiting for me in the church."

He rose from his chair. "Have you volunteered for the committee?"

"I have. I find it best to keep busy." She held her new notebook against her bosom as she retreated to the door. "Good afternoon, Mark. And thank you again."

Chapter Five

Mark wasn't used to being disliked. He'd had a few minor difficulties with people over the course of his life, it was true, but as a whole, he generally got along with everyone. It was a fact which made Ernest's animosity toward him a bit difficult to accept.

Then again, Ernest wasn't exactly a person.

Attached to a loose rope lead, the cantankerous little dog had snarled and snapped at Mark's trouser leg the entire walk to the Grange. Mark was certain he'd find a bruise on his ankle when he returned to the vicarage. For a dog with snaggled teeth, Ernest could deliver a surprisingly effective bite.

Mark sat down on one of the old stone benches in the Grange's rose garden. An arbor stood over it, sagging slightly under the weight of the climbing roses that covered it. He'd told the housekeeper he'd be waiting there. With any luck, Ernest would show to better effect in the outdoors. He lay down on the grass as they waited, intermittently flashing a threatening canine glare in Mark's direction.

"I'd be your friend if you'd let me," Mark said to him.

Ernest responded with a muffled growl.

"Suit yourself." Mark settled back on the bench and waited. He took comfort in the fact that, on the few occasions they'd met, Ernest had seemed to like Beryl. Granted, it had been over a year ago, but Mark had high hopes the little dog would remember her.

Beryl didn't keep them waiting long. Not five minutes later, she came walking across the lawn, wearing a white muslin day dress with a green ribbon sash at her waist. A wide-brimmed straw hat hung in her hand.

Mark stood to greet her, his heart beating hard. It was ridiculous. He'd had an entire year to master his feelings in her absence. And he'd truly believed that he had. He and Beryl were friends. The humorous letters he'd written to her had solidified that relationship. Friends who were soon to be related by marriage.

Why then did his pulse still race whenever he saw her? Why did his heart lurch and his neck grow warm beneath his cravat?

And what about two days ago in his office at the church?

He'd come within an inch of taking her in his arms. She'd been so close—her hand flat on his chest and her skirts crushed against his legs. His breath had stopped. The *world* had stopped.

By some miracle, he'd had the presence of mind to ask her to move away from him. To recall himself to his sense of duty. But it had been a very near thing. He wondered if she realized just how near.

He thought not.

Beryl had never seemed to realize anything about his feelings for her at all. He fell too easily into the role of friend. Of village curate, there to advise and comfort. It would never occur to her to look at him in that way. The way she looked at Henry.

But no.

She'd never looked at Henry that way either, had she? Mark had seen them holding hands on the day their betrothal was announced, and Henry had often taken Beryl driving or for strolls in the garden. But the two of them hadn't evinced any level of passionate affection for each other. There had been no long looks. No lingering touches. None that Mark had observed.

"Mrs. Witherspoon told me you'd come to call," Beryl said. "Why didn't you wait in the drawing room?"

Beside him, Ernest jumped to his feet and started barking.

"Ah, I see." She smiled. "Is that Mrs. Arbuthnot's dog?"

"Ernest," Mark said. "Do you remember him?"

"Of course I do." Beryl sank down in front of the little dog and offered him her hand. She wasn't wearing gloves. Her bare fingers were slim and elegant. Unbearably feminine. Mark recalled how they'd felt, resting on his chest. How he'd wanted to cover them with his own hand. To hold them safe.

Ernest immediately ceased barking. He sniffed at her hand before cautiously approaching and permitting her to stroke his head. His plumed tail wagged slowly, looking rather like a bedraggled black ostrich feather swaying in the breeze.

"Ernest," she said, scratching his chin. "What a handsome fellow you are." She glanced up at Mark. Her hair was caught up in a plaited roll at her nape. A few golden strands had come loose to curl alongside her cheek and temple. "Why do you have him?"

"Mrs. Arbuthnot left this morning. She's gone to live with her daughter and son-in-law."

"And Ernest wasn't welcome, is that it?" She scooped the little dog up in her arms. He made no protest. "Poor thing. What shall become of you?"

"As to that…" Mark cleared his throat. Suddenly, it no longer seemed like such a good idea. Seeing Beryl with Ernest—she with her fine dress and her golden beauty, and he with his snaggled teeth and less than appealing pedigree—was eye-opening, to say the least. Could a pair have ever appeared more ill-suited?

But beauty had little to do with happiness. And, after all, handsome or ugly, Ernest still had something Beryl needed.

"I thought you might take him," Mark said.

Beryl sank down onto the bench. "Me?"

Mark took a seat at her side, closer than he'd intended. So close that her skirts bunched against his leg. "You haven't any pets. And I know you're fond of animals. He would be good for you, I think. And you… Well, it's no exaggeration to say that you'd be saving his life." He explained about Ernest's impending appointment with Mrs. Doolittle and her chloroform.

Beryl looked appalled. "How horrid. You wouldn't let her destroy him, would you?"

"There's little I can do on his behalf, save try to find him a home. I'd take him myself, but he can't stand the sight of me."

"He's afraid of gentlemen." Beryl settled Ernest on her lap. "Didn't Mrs. Arbuthnot explain?"

Mark's brows knit. "Afraid? Why should he be?"

"Many little dogs are. I daresay it's because you're all so big and threatening. He only needs to learn that you won't hurt him." She reached out. "Here. Give me your hand." She didn't wait for permission. Her fingers closed around his, drawing his hand across her lap.

A jolt of heat went through him. He had to remind himself to keep breathing as she clasped his bare hand in hers and very gently maneuvered his fingers to pet Ernest's back.

"There," she murmured to Ernest. "You see? Mark won't hurt you. He's your friend."

Mark swallowed hard. Until that moment, he hadn't fully registered the privacy of their location. Climbing roses swathed the back of the arbor and drooped down the sides, enveloping them in soft perfume, and partially shielding them from view. It gave their meeting a feeling of romance. As if they were a courting couple who had stolen away for a secret embrace.

But they weren't a couple, courting or otherwise.

He reminded himself of that fact, even as Beryl's touch sent a minor earthquake through his heart. "Precisely what I've been telling him."

Ernest gave him a doubtful look. His bewhiskered lips twitched as if he was contemplating another snarl, but no snarl was forthcoming.

Mark lifted his gaze from the little dog to say something to Beryl. Some careless remark to disguise the warmth in his blood and the erratic rhythm of his pulse. He expected her to appear as oblivious to the effect she had on him as always. But she didn't.

She wasn't.

A flush of pink, as delicate as a damask rose petal, had crept up her pale throat and into her cheeks.

His heart slammed against his ribs. It was all he could do to keep his countenance. Good lord. She was *blushing*.

And it was because of him. Because she was holding his hand.

His fingers curled instinctively around hers. "Beryl, I—"

She spoke at the same time. "Mark, why did you—"

They both broke off. The tension between them was palpable.

"Forgive me," he said gruffly. "You go first."

Beryl's gaze dropped from Mark's to settle on Ernest. The little dog had made himself comfortable in her lap, curling up in a tiny ball. And beside him, her hand settled in Mark's much larger one. Warm and safe. It felt like the most natural thing in the world.

And the most exciting.

Her heart was fluttering, and her face had warmed with a self-conscious heat. "Why did you say that he would be good for me?"

Mark was quiet a moment. "Because of something you told me that day by the riverbank. I don't mean to remind you—"

"It's all right." She supposed she should have released his hand. She was no longer introducing him to Ernest. But she wasn't yet ready to lose the comfort of Mark's grasp, and he seemed in no hurry to let her go. "What did I say?"

"That, at its worst, the melancholy you experience is akin to feeling alone and unloved."

"It is, unfortunately." She could think of no better way to describe it. That feeling of sadness that encroached in her vulnerable moments. She'd been attempting to evade it for years. By taking up various charitable tasks. By visiting sick villagers, or volunteering for various ladies' committees. As if, by keeping busy, she could outrun it somehow.

And then night would come, or those early hours in the morning, still abed as the first glints of sunlight shone through her chintz curtains. It was in those moments of stillness that the sadness preyed on her the worst. Then, there was no way to escape it.

Mark's thumb moved over her knuckles in a reassuring caress. "I've been thinking about it a lot," he said. "Thinking about you."

She slowly lifted her gaze back to his. She was surprised by the warmth she found in his eyes. By the way the color had seemed to change—to darken.

Odd that.

All these years, she'd thought Mark's eyes were the same shade of blue as Henry's. But that wasn't true at all. Where Henry's were hard as sapphire, Mark's were soft as velvet. A warm, saturated blue, like the wildflowers on the banks of the Worthy.

She inhaled an unsteady breath. Her new French corset must be laced too tightly. It was compressing her vitals, making her insides go tight and trembly. "You've taken my problem very much to heart."

"Of course, I have. You're my—" A slight pause. "You're my friend. I think the world of you, Beryl."

"I think the world of you, too," she said. "I missed you in Paris." The words came before she had the good sense to stop them. "I miss you now, on the days that I don't see you. You were right about my needing someone to talk to."

Mark was always right. It's what made him so good at his job. He always knew just what to say and what to do to make someone feel comforted. It was his gift. She wasn't anyone special. And yet…

Sitting with him now, holding his hand, she very much felt as if she might be.

"Have you tried writing in your journal?" he asked.

"I have." She'd made a concerted effort. It had been awkward at first, scratching away with her quill pen, uncertain of where to begin. But over the past two days, her random jottings had transformed into a record of her private thoughts and feelings. Of the petty frustrations she sometimes felt with her family, and the secret misgivings she had in relation to her upcoming marriage.

It seemed a betrayal to record such unhappy reflections when she knew very well she had nothing to complain about. So much so, that she'd taken to hiding her journal beneath her mattress right alongside her copy of the *Provincial Medical and Surgical Gazette*.

"Has it helped at all?

"A little," she said. "I wish I could say it's cured me, but I don't think it can. And, as dear as Ernest is, I don't believe he can either. I'm sorry, but—"

He pressed her hand. "You've misread my intentions. I have no expectation of curing you. I only want you to have things to better help you cope when the melancholy preys on your spirits. You've said you feel alone and unloved. Well… now you'll have Ernest with you."

"Oh, Mark…"

"It's common sense, really. How can you feel unloved when there's someone with you who loves you so devotedly? Or will love you, I hope. Only look at him. He's already halfway there."

Beryl set her free hand on Ernest's narrow back. The little dog was curled up tight, practically clinging to her. No doubt he was missing Mrs. Arbuthnot. He'd need all the comfort and affection he could get in the coming days. "Very well," Beryl said. "I'll keep him. But I warn you, the sight of him is going to have my mother sending for her smelling salts."

Mark had no opportunity to answer, for in that same moment, Winnifred came bounding up the lawn.

She was in her riding habit, her heavy skirts draped over one arm. Her head was bare, her fair hair half-falling from its pins. "Beryl!" she called breathlessly. "There you are. I've been looking all over for you."

Beryl's hand slipped free from Mark's as she shot to her feet, still holding Ernest safe in her arms. Her gaze swept over Winnifred's dirt-stained habit and disheveled hair. "What's happened? You're not hurt, are you?"

"Goodness, no. I've only been out riding."

"Then what—"

"It's the post. Mama insists you come at once. An enormous box has arrived from Paris. Aunt Hortensia is certain it's your wedding dress."

Mark stood beside Beryl. She could sense him there, tense and quiet. Only seconds before, she'd been holding his hand, as intimately as she'd ever held Henry's. More intimately, for Henry's touch had never made her heart beat faster. And it had certainly never made her blush.

"Winnifred, your timing is—"

"Yes, yes, but you must make haste. Mama demands that you try the dress on directly. If it needs additional alterations, Aunt Hortensia says it will have to be sent up to London." Winnifred caught Beryl's arm, only belatedly registering the presence of Ernest. "Good grief. Is that Mrs. Arbuthnot's ugly little dog?"

"He's *not* ugly," Beryl said. "And he's my dog now." She cast an apologetic glance at Mark as her sister pulled her away. "Forgive the interruption."

"Not at all." Mark smiled. "This is a special occasion, is it not? The arrival of your wedding dress. You must go, of course."

There was a peculiar undercurrent to his words. A gossamer thread of emotion that Beryl couldn't identify. It made his voice sound vaguely stiff, and his smile seem almost wooden. She gave him a searching look.

"You can stay if you like," Winnifred offered magnanimously. "It's only the groom who can't see her in her dress before the wedding. And you're not the groom. You're merely his brother. There's no bad luck associated with that, surely."

"No, indeed. No bad luck at all." Mark picked up his hat from the stone bench. He smoothed the nap of it with his sleeve, a strangely somber expression passing over his face. "Regrettably, I'm needed at the vicarage." He took his leave from them then with a bow, more formal than was his habit. "Good afternoon, ladies."

"He was in a queer mood," Winnifred remarked as she and Beryl returned to the house. "I trust it wasn't something I said."

Chapter Six

Mark dropped the stack of books he was carrying onto the lace-draped walnut console table in the vicarage's entry hall. *The Posthumous Papers of the Pickwick Club*, his well-worn Bible, and an equally worn copy of Wordsworth's *Lyrical Ballads*.

He'd been calling on parishioners all morning. Two of the most elderly residents of the village were consigned to their beds with influenza. Another was suffering with gout. And yet another, Mrs. Priddy, had recently been abandoned by her drunken lout of a husband and was sorely in need of comfort.

Mark had visited them all, taking as much time with them as they needed. Longer, perhaps, than he usually might have done. He felt no particular urgency to return to his office in the church. No desire to encounter the ladies' committee preparing for the summer fete.

They'd been bustling about all week. It wasn't uncommon for him to encounter them several times throughout the day.

Beryl was a member of the committee now.

He'd seen her only once since their encounter in the Grange's rose garden two days ago. She'd been walking along the green outside his office window in the company of Mrs. Malvern, Ernest cradled under one arm. A smile had crept up on Mark as he'd looked at her. The picture she made with that wretched little dog. It had warmed his heart, even as it twisted it to the point of pain.

No. He wasn't eager to return to the church. To see her again, however accidentally. He needed a short moment of respite.

But it wasn't to be.

No sooner had he entered the hall than Mrs. Phillips approached, her lace-trimmed cap askew on her snow-white hair. "Mr. Rivenhall. Thank heaven you've returned. Sir Henry came to call. I told him you wouldn't be back before two o'clock."

"Oh?" Mark removed his hat and gloves. "How long ago did he leave?"

"That's just it, sir. He hasn't left. He's still here. In the parlor, taking tea with Mr. Venable."

Mark went still. Henry was here? Impossible. He never came to visit. Not if he could help it. He had too many demands on his time. A whole list of important items requiring his attention. If Mark was on the list at all, he was at the very bottom of it.

"I see." He straightened his waistcoat. "I suppose I'd better join them."

Mr. Venable's warbly voice emerged from the parlor as Mark approached. "Not in my time, sir," he was saying. "Nor in any that I can recall."

"Times do change," Henry replied. "But I agree. I like straying from the traditions no more than you do." He looked up as Mark entered the room. "At last. My brother has returned."

"Henry." Mark inclined his head. "Venable. Glad to see you're feeling a bit better."

There was a fire in the hearth, blazing at full force. Mr. Venable's velvet wingback chair was arranged close to it. He had a woolen blanket draped across his lap and another drawn around his shoulders. "Always pleased to welcome a distinguished guest."

Henry returned his teacup to the tea tray, rising from his seat on the sofa before Mark could take a seat himself. "I'm afraid I've overtaxed you."

"Not at all, sir. Not at all." Mr. Venable fell into a bout of coughing. He pressed his handkerchief to his mouth until it passed.

Mark watched him carefully. He was suffering badly from consumption. His skin was waxen, his features drawn with pain and fatigue. "Shall I fetch Mrs. Phillips?"

"Unnecessary," Mr. Venable wheezed. "I'm perfectly well, as you see."

"I will bid you good day, then," Henry said, bowing. "Mark? If I can trouble you to walk me out?"

Mark reluctantly obliged him. As they crossed through the hall, he exchanged a weighted glance with Mrs. Phillips. She gave him a nod of understanding before hurrying into the parlor. Mr. Venable might not be willing to admit he needed help—not in front of a man like Henry—but Mark recognized when the old vicar was struggling.

"Will you take a turn about the grounds with me?" Henry asked.

"If you like." Mark followed his brother out, shutting the front door of the vicarage behind them. "Any particular reason?"

"I came here to speak with you, not to have a tea party with an invalid. Another quarter of an hour and I'd have gone."

"I didn't see your carriage."

"I walked from the Park."

Mark's mouth hitched in a humorless smile. "A rarity."

"It's a pleasant enough day for it. Not that you'd know it from the inferno in your parlor." Henry gave him a dry look. "Does Venable always keep the vicarage at such a temperature?"

"He's dying."

"So I gather." A long pause. "He mentioned retirement."

Mark walked alongside Henry into the small wilderness garden that lay adjacent to the vicarage. Shade trees grew there at odd angles, and colorful weeds sprouted as readily as the wildflowers that blanketed the ground. It was a secluded enough spot, filtered by light and shadow. Mark often strolled there in the early hours of the morning, or after dinner, as dusk was falling, when he needed to think, or to pray.

It was strange to be walking here with his brother of all people. Henry had never been a man prone to reflection.

"I believe he's beginning to take the prospect seriously," Mark said. "But he's still resistant to the idea. He doesn't wish to give up his church. Which is understandable, given the length of his tenure."

"It's my church," Henry said. "And you're already vicar here in all but name."

"Is that what you wanted to talk with me about? You've made some sort of decision about my future?" *Again.* Mark didn't say the word aloud, but he may as well have done. It hung there in the air between them.

"You take pleasure in painting me as a villain," Henry said. "Someone had to take things in hand after our father died."

Their father, the late Sir Richard Rivenhall, had been a profligate. He'd drunk and gambled the family fortune away, leaving the estate on the brink of ruin. If not for Henry's tenacity—his single-minded stubbornness and determination—Rivenhall Park would have been sold years ago. Instead, Henry had resurrected it by sheer force of will. It was now once again the jewel of Shepton Worthy. And Henry himself, the matrimonial prize of Somerset.

At least, he had been up until the day his betrothal was announced.

Mark's expression hardened to recall it. "It has nothing to do with our father—"

"And you haven't done too badly in the bargain," Henry went on, talking straight over him. "Unless, of course, you're still nurturing some longing to be a soldier?"

Mark thrust his hands into the pockets of his trousers. No. He had no desire to be a soldier. Such dreams had been the stuff of his youth. Even then, they'd been little more than rebellion against the iron will of his older brother.

From birth, Mark had been destined for the church, just as Jack had been destined for the army. It had always been thus with the second and third sons in their family for too many generations to count. Mark had understood that. In time, he'd come to accept it.

"Of course not," he said.

"Exactly so. I've never met a man more suited to the clergy. If I'd have succumbed to your pleading and bought you a commission— Well." Henry's mouth flattened. "I daresay you'd be as dead as Jack right now."

Mark's chest tightened. "Don't use Jack's death to win an old quarrel."

They walked in silence for several steps before Henry spoke again. "I sometimes wonder what he'd have had to say about this distance between us."

Mark didn't reply. Not at first. He couldn't. Jack had been gone a year. The pain of his loss had lessened, but the emptiness left by his death was a pain in itself. He'd been the glue that had held Mark and Henry together. Without him, it sometimes felt as if there was nothing left between them but hurt and recrimination.

And jealousy.

Mark was ashamed to admit it, even to himself. "He wouldn't be surprised. Jack knew how difficult you could be."

"Because I didn't allow him to squander his money? Didn't permit him to marry that farmer's daughter when he was eighteen, or to set up that music hall singer as his mistress when he was twenty?" Henry kicked at a stone in his path. It skittered off into the underbrush. "Jack was wild for a time. He needed taking in hand."

"*I* wasn't wild."

"Not wild, no. But you haven't always known what's in your best interests."

A cloud drifted past the sun, briefly darkening the path in front of them.

"It seems to me," Mark said in a voice of creditable calm, "that you have a strangely self-serving way of calculating what's best for people."

Henry's shoulders stiffened. They were perilously close to an argument. And Henry despised arguments. He had no tolerance for passionate displays of any kind. "Have you ever had reason to question my judgment?" he asked. "Every decision I've ever made has been proved out in the end. Rivenhall Park is evidence enough of that."

Mark felt a rare flash of pity for his brother. "Human emotion is rather more complicated than the workings of a country estate. You can't tally it up in a ledger. It doesn't always balance the way you expect it to."

"It balances. If one is disciplined enough." Circumstances had obliged Henry to be disciplined. He was almost soldierly in that regard, more so than Jack had ever been. "You think me unfeeling," he said, "but I've always tried to look after you."

"I know you have," Mark admitted. "Though I sometimes question the way you go about it."

"We each have our talents. Yours is for listening, and being compassionate. And mine is for recognizing hard truths. For choosing the right course and staying it."

Mark gave him a look. "You might *try* listening on occasion."

"I listen enough. But in the end, I must do what's right for those within my power, though it may make some revile me for it."

Mark was tempted to laugh. "I don't revile you. That would take too much effort."

Henry's mouth twitched. A threat of a smile. "Not you. Miss Winnifred."

Mark's brows lifted. "What have you done to get in her black books?"

"Nothing yet. But I'll be selling that horse she's been riding. The one she's grown so fond of. It can't be helped." Henry's features settled back into a frown. "He unseated her on the road."

Mark came to an abrupt halt. "Is she all right?"

Henry stopped. "She's fine. A little shaken, the groom said. But not troubled enough by the event to tell me about it herself. It happened days ago."

Mark recalled the disheveled appearance Winnifred had presented at the Grange when she'd come to fetch her sister from the garden. "She was probably too embarrassed to admit to it. She prides herself on her riding skill, and with good reason."

"She has too much pride," Henry said. "Too much reckless confidence. She'll break her neck one of these days."

"Is the horse that dangerous?"

"He's suitable enough for a man. But he's not meant for a lady. I'm sending him up to London next week for the sales. I'll get a better price there."

"You'll break her heart."

"She'll get over it." Henry resumed walking. "Her mother and sister will thank me in the end."

Mark sighed. He caught up with his brother in two strides. "Does it never occur to you that sometimes you don't know best? That on occasion, all you're doing is running over people and giving them a dislike of you?"

Henry shot him a dangerous glance. "Are you speaking of someone in particular?"

"Don't be absurd. I'm only remarking that, sometimes, it might benefit you to listen to people, and to try to understand. Especially where ladies are concerned."

"I more than comprehend you."

"I'm quite sure that you don't." Mark looked straight ahead as they walked. "I'm not talking about *her*."

Henry was quiet for a tension-filled moment. "You've been seeing a lot of her."

"Naturally. She's on the ladies' committee for the summer fete." *And she's my friend.*

But Mark didn't say that. He didn't have to. They both knew what Beryl was to him. It was the very cause of the rift between them.

Though Mark couldn't blame it all on his unrequited feelings.

He and Henry had never been particularly close. They were too different, each the polar opposite of the other. They might have gone on that way forever, calling an uneasy truce as many brothers do. But Henry had insisted on asserting himself. On courting her. Proposing to her.

Mark's own feelings for Beryl had been dismissed as easily as Henry dismissed any other obstacle in his path.

"Why did you come here today?" Mark asked. "You must have had some reason."

"To talk with you about your future. As I said, you're already vicar here in all but name." Henry clasped his hands at his back. His face was hard. Unreadable. "When Venable retires, I suppose you'll be expecting me to formally grant you the living."

A frisson of foreboding jolted Mark's gaze to his brother's. Their eyes locked. "That's always been the plan, hasn't it? It's the reason I've stayed on so long as curate."

"Plans can change."

Understanding sank in. With it came a simmering anger, the likes of which Mark had never felt toward Henry before. "You're threatening to take the church away from me."

"I'm not threatening anything," Henry said calmly. "I'd merely like you to consider whether, after my marriage, you might not be happier somewhere else."

Chapter Seven

*B*eryl settled back into the velvet seat cushions of Aunt Hortensia's carriage. Ernest was curled snugly upon her lap. It had been only a few days since Mark had brought him to the Grange. During that time, the little dog had attached himself to Beryl with a desperate canine determination. He'd taken to following her wherever she went, and if prohibited from accompanying her, would cry most piteously.

"You shouldn't indulge the creature," Aunt Hortensia said. Seated across from Beryl in the carriage, she was decked out in her Sunday best, the plumes of her bonnet nearly brushing the ceiling.

"He's grieving the loss of his old mistress," Beryl replied. "It would be a cruelty to leave him behind."

"A catastrophe as well," Mama said from her place next to Aunt Hortensia. "He's the untidiest creature I've ever encountered. Did Mrs. Arbuthnot never think to teach him better manners?"

Beryl set a protective hand on Ernest's back. "I'm sure he knows how to behave. He's only a little unreliable at present. I expect it's because of his change in circumstance."

Winnifred was beside Beryl in the carriage, the silk skirts of her best Sunday dress billowing wide over a wire crinoline. "Yes, I daresay it was an excess of grief that made him soil the sofa leg last night."

Mama looked pained. "I pray that Mrs. Witherspoon will be able to remove the stain. The drawing room carpet is in poor enough condition without—"

"Enough," Aunt Hortensia said. "We'll speak no more of the dog's despicable habits."

"Your aunt is right. It isn't at all a suitable subject for Sunday conversation." Mama's gaze lit on Ernest, her face making a moue of disapproval. "You'll leave him in the carriage, of course."

Aunt Hortensia puffed up. "Not in my carriage, she won't. The little beast can be tied to the churchyard fence, where he can do no harm."

"Poor Ernest," Winnifred said as the carriage rolled to a halt in front of the church. "Reduced to relieving himself out of doors."

"Winnifred, really," Mama said.

"It's only for an hour." Beryl scratched Ernest's head. "And I do think he'll prefer it to being left at the Grange. At least here, he'll be able to see where I've gone."

The footman opened the carriage door and lowered the step. He handed Aunt Hortensia and Mama down first, before assisting Winnifred.

Beryl climbed out last. While her family was occupied in greeting some of the villagers at the church gate, she carried

Ernest to a section of the churchyard away from the main path. Sinking down onto the ground, she secured his lead to the fencepost in a loose knot.

"Good boy," she said, giving him one final pat before rejoining the others.

Ernest watched her go. He didn't whine or howl in protest. For the moment, he seemed content to lie down upon the grass.

Ahead, Mark stood at the door of the church. He was in his clerical collar, cassock, and surplice, his mouth tilted in a smile as he addressed one of the families entering the vestibule. Mr. Venable was at his side, waxen and frail.

Beryl studied him with concern. He looked terribly ill.

"Mrs. Burnham. Mrs. Sheldrake." Mark inclined his head to Mama and Aunt Hortensia.

"Good morning, Mr. Rivenhall," Mama said. "And to you, Mr. Venable. I trust you're feeling a little better?"

As Mama and Aunt Hortensia spoke with the vicar, Winnifred pressed forward to address Mark. "Has your brother arrived?"

"He's already inside."

"Splendid." Winnifred plunged through the crowd to enter the church.

Mark met Beryl's eyes. His smile seemed to falter. "Miss Burnham."

Beryl was suddenly conscious of the people around them. There was no privacy, no more than when she'd last encountered Mark at the church. "Mr. Rivenhall."

"You're well?"

"Quite well." She wanted to say something more. To tell him that he'd been right about Ernest, just as he'd been right about the journal. To say that she missed sitting with him. Talking with him.

But there was no opportunity.

Mama and Aunt Hortensia moved into the vestibule, and Beryl had no choice but to accompany them.

Mama took Beryl's arm as they advanced up the aisle. "Mr. Venable is giving the sermon this morning, poor fellow. One wonders why he would bestir himself. Unless...do you suppose he's announcing his retirement?"

Beryl hadn't the faintest idea. "Do you think he might?"

"It's past time he did," Mama said. "I'll have a word with Sir Henry about it next time he comes for dinner."

Henry was seated in the Rivenhall family pew at the front of the church. Winnifred was at his side, speaking to him in an animated fashion. Her cheeks were flushed, her eyes peculiarly bright.

If Beryl didn't know better, she might think the pair of them were engaged in a heated argument. But Henry showed no sign of ill humor. He was calm and controlled as ever, listening to Winnifred in complete silence.

At the sight of Beryl and her mother approaching, he stood to greet them. "Miss Burnham. Mrs. Burnham."

"Sir Henry." Mama gave Winnifred a questioning glance.

"Is something the matter?" Beryl asked.

"Nothing that can be solved here," Winnifred said tightly.

"Henry?" Beryl looked to him for an answer.

"Your sister's right," he said. "Not here."

Mama set a hand on Winnifred's shoulder. "Come, my dear. We must return to our seat before the service starts."

Winnifred grudgingly got up and moved with them to the pew behind Sir Henry's. Aunt Hortensia was already there, examining the church decorations through the lenses of her lorgnette.

"Are you responsible for this?" she asked as Beryl sat down next to her. "All this floral nonsense?"

Clusters of greenery, wildflowers, and ribbons hung at the end of each pew. A delicate, eminently tasteful decoration. Beryl had spent an entire afternoon affixing them, and was rather pleased with how they looked. "You don't like them?"

"Can't see any point in such fripperies. Not inside a church."

"They're the same flowers and ribbons the ladies' committee is using to decorate the stalls at the fete."

Aunt Hortensia gave a grunt of disapproval. "Commerce."

"It isn't commerce. It's charity. Everything the villagers sell at the fete was made with their own hands, and all of the proceeds go to help the church." Beryl had spent most of her life in Shepton Worthy volunteering for such events. It was how she'd kept her mind occupied. How she'd kept the melancholy at bay.

Indeed, she'd often suspected that it was this very propensity for charitable endeavors that had first attracted Henry's notice. That he'd seen her doggedly visiting the sick and helping to raise funds for the church and concluded that she was perfectly suited to be the wife of a country baronet. A lady who would engage in appropriate activities—who wasn't prone to silliness or excess, but instead devoted to the well-being of others.

And she *did* care about the villagers and the church, about the sick and the needy. But her work on various committees wasn't altruistic. It was selfish. A means of combating a private demon.

No one knew that, because no one knew *her*. No one but Mark.

She gazed up at him as the service started. He was clothed as soberly as Mr. Venable, but unlike the vicar—or any clergyman Beryl had encountered before—Mark looked startlingly handsome in his clerical garments. He was tall and broad-shouldered, his dark hair attractively rumpled, though he must have recently combed it.

He'd been running his fingers through it again. It was a sure sign that he was distracted. Troubled, even. That, and the uncommon solemnity in his blue eyes.

She wondered what was wrong.

Whatever it was, it didn't inhibit his reading of the scripture. His voice was steady and thoughtful as he read a passage from the Old Testament. When he'd finished, he led them in a psalm before making way for Mr. Venable at the carved walnut pulpit.

The vicar cleared his throat several times before beginning his sermon with a wheezing passage from John: "'A woman, when she is in travail, hath sorrow…'"

Five minutes dragged into ten. Beryl's mind was just beginning to wander when her attention was arrested by the queerest sound. It was coming from the back of the church. An odd hissing noise that stopped and started several times, growing ever closer.

From his seat in the chancel, Mark glanced down the aisle. A look of almost comical dismay came over his face.

Beryl turned in her seat to follow his gaze. Her eyes widened in horror.

It was Ernest. His lead dragging behind him, he was making his way to her up the aisle, stopping intermittently to lift his hind leg against the greenery that hung on the end of the pews.

Mark gave a choked cough.

Beryl didn't dare meet his eyes. She rose from her seat in a flash, strode down the aisle and swept Ernest up in her arms and straight out of the church.

She carried him into the churchyard, the vicar's sermon trailing behind them on the morning breeze. He must not have seen Ernest—or heard him. Beryl prayed no one else had either.

"You naughty, naughty little dog," she whispered. "To have done such a thing, and in a church of all places. Have you no sense of decency?"

Ernest gave her cheek a penitent lick.

A gurgle of laughter rose in her chest. She bit her cheek to stifle it. If Mama or Aunt Hortensia followed her out, it wouldn't do for them to find her giggling at such vulgar behavior.

But moments later, it wasn't her mother or aunt who appeared around the side of the church. It was Mark. He was still in his cassock and surplice.

"Oh no," she said. "Have I disrupted the service?"

He shook his head. Suppressed mirth gleamed in his eyes. "I slipped out through the side door. No one else appears to have noticed a thing."

"Not even the villagers at the back?"

"Not that I could tell. Most were looking at Venable. The rest were half asleep."

She dropped Ernest down on the grass. "I'm dreadfully sorry. I thought I'd tied him securely. I'd no idea he would get loose—or that he'd behave in such a dishonorable fashion."

"It's I who should be apologizing. I'm the one who gave you the dog."

"With the best of intentions. And you were right. He's been such a comfort to me. Though, I must admit, his habits aren't as fastidious as one might wish."

Mark choked back a sound of amusement. "A vast under-statement."

Her own laughter bubbled to the surface. "The look on your face."

"And on yours. It was all I could do to smother a laugh."

"I don't know why you should be laughing. What he did was next door to sacrilege." But she was laughing, too. Indeed, she laughed so much, that tears sprang to her eyes. She had to lean against the wall of the church to keep from doubling over with it.

Mark was equally afflicted. He propped next to her on the wall, overcome with hilarity. "Mrs. Arbuthnot did say he was prone to messiness. I hadn't realized she was referencing his plumbing."

"Oh, do stop." Beryl clutched a hand to her corseted waist. "You're giving me a stitch in my side."

"Forgive me," he said, still grinning. "It's not really even that funny, is it?"

She swiped at her eyes. "Indeed. We should both be appalled."

"Just so." Standing from the wall, he ran a hand through his hair. He gave her a rueful smile. "I'd best get back before the sermon ends."

But he didn't go. Quite the reverse. He came closer, and reaching up, brushed his fingers gently against her cheek. His expression softened. Not with humor this time, but with some-thing else. Something warmer and infinitely tender.

"I haven't seen this dimple in an age," he said.

Beryl's heart thumped hard. Her mouth was still curved in a smile, but the hilarity of the moment had gone. It was replaced by a peculiar tension. A deep thread of connection, vibrating between them, just as it had when she'd sat next to him in the Grange's rose garden. Drawing her closer to him, almost against her will.

Impulsively, she covered his hand with hers, and turning her head, brushed her lips against his palm.

Mark made a sound low in his throat. "Beryl, I—"

"Don't say anything."

They were neither of them smiling now.

He gave her a searching look, and then slowly, slowly bent his head to hers. She stretched up to meet him, her breath trembling out of her as Mark's arm slid around her waist and his mouth captured hers.

She'd been kissed before. A brief kiss from Henry on the day of their betrothal. It had been everything that was chaste and proper. Utterly unobjectionable. But that kiss had been a different manner of thing. A fleeting exchange between two restrained individuals.

This was something else entirely.

Mark kissed her softly, deeply. An intimate kiss that left nothing secret. It made her heart stop and start again. Made her knees go weak, and her body flush with unexpected heat.

She clutched at the fabric of his surplice.

His *surplice*.

The reality of it jolted her back to her senses as effectively as a bucket of ice water. Heavens above. She was kissing the curate of Shepton Worthy. Mark Rivenhall. The man who was soon to be her brother-in-law.

Wrenching her mouth from his, she broke free of his arms. Her back met the stone wall of the church, her chest constricting on a panting breath. Oh lord, what had she done?

What had she done?

Mark stared down at her, stunned. His blood was still simmering, his breath as unsteady as her own. He reached out to her. "Beryl, wait."

She turned away from him, her fingers lifting to her lips. She looked slightly dazed. "What have I done?"

He didn't know if she was posing the whispered question to him or to herself. He answered it anyway. "It was my fault. I shouldn't have—"

"I could have stopped you."

"You *did* stop me."

"Yes. Too late." Her eyes found his, her face stricken. "And now I've ruined everything."

Had she ripped Mark's heart from his chest and trod on it, she couldn't have crushed his spirits more effectively. Here he was, senses still throbbing from their kiss, and all she could think about was her betrothal to Henry.

But of course she would. And how could he blame her? Henry wasn't the third party in this relationship. It was Mark himself. He was the sinner, not the one who'd just been sinned against.

If kissing Beryl could ever be called a sin.

It had been the single most glorious experience of his life. The culmination of years of longing. That brief, clinging moment of shared heat and breath. Her soft lips shaping and yielding to his. They'd fit together so perfectly.

But she belonged to Henry.

A surge of bitter resentment took Mark unaware. He did his best to suppress it. "Nothing's ruined. Henry need never know of it."

"You would condone lying to him?"

"No, but—" He forced himself to say the words. "What we did… It didn't mean anything."

It was the furthest thing from the truth. Their kiss had meant everything to him. But he wouldn't have her feeling guilty over it, believing that she'd betrayed Henry—that she'd committed some unpardonable sin.

Beryl made a soft sound. He couldn't interpret it. She'd turned away from him, her face hidden from view.

"Your reputation is unharmed," he added. "No one observed us. And it won't happen again. We both know that. It was a stupid mistake. I see no reason for us to upset Henry for nothing."

She walked a few steps away from him, arms folded at her waist. Ernest was curled up on the grass nearby. He raised his head to watch her.

In the distance, Mr. Venable's frail voice rang out as his sermon reached a crescendo.

They had no real privacy here. Indeed, it was a miracle they'd been left alone thus far.

Mark raked his fingers through his hair. He vaguely registered that his hand was shaking. "I have to get back. My absence will be remarked."

She nodded. "Yes. Of course." Her voice was strange. "I'll take Ernest to the carriage."

He didn't offer to accompany her. He didn't have the strength to prolong their encounter.

Straightening his surplice, he reentered the church through the side door and quietly returned to his seat in the chancel.

The congregation was still sitting in their pews, just as they'd been when Mark had gone. Everything looked the same. He nevertheless felt as though he'd entered a different world. Not because of them, but because of *him*. Kissing Beryl had changed him irrevocably. Had made him viscerally aware of the impossibility of continuing on as he was.

Henry had been right, as always. Had recognized the difficulty of the situation before Mark fully appreciated it himself. He couldn't stay in Shepton Worthy after Beryl was married. He couldn't be around her anymore and not have her.

Chapter Eight

The carriage ride home was a subdued affair. Beryl sat silent beside an equally silent Winnifred. It was only Mama who spoke, her words of reprimand about Ernest punctuated by those from Aunt Hortensia.

"To have relieved himself inside of the church!" Mama closed her eyes in mortification "Had I known that was why you left so abruptly during the service, I'd have been too embarrassed to remain myself."

"Pray that no one else observed the foul deed," Aunt Hortensia said unhelpfully.

Mama paled at the prospect.

"No one saw," Beryl said at last. No one save Mark. But she didn't dare mention him. Her feelings about what had happened between the two of them were still too strange. Too raw. "I shall go straight back after changing my dress and replace the greenery myself."

The prospect made her a trifle queasy. She'd no doubt encounter Mark again. It was too soon. She didn't wish to see him until she'd had time to think.

"I can't fathom why Mr. Rivenhall would have given you such a creature," Mama continued, unmollified. "And I shall never understand what prompted you to accept him. If you desired a lapdog, you could have waited for Sir Henry to provide one. A handsome little spaniel, perhaps. Or even a pug. Something more pleasing to the eye."

Beryl's arms tightened around Ernest. He was perched in her lap, unaffected by the aspersions cast on his character and appearance. She didn't exert herself to defend him. She had more important things on her mind at present than Ernest's unfortunate behavior at the church.

When the carriage stopped at the front steps of the Grange, she was the first one out, making her way upstairs to her bedroom without a word. Once there, she closed the door behind her and dropped Ernest onto the quilt at the foot of her bed.

There was no point in summoning Mary to help her undress. Beryl's silk bodice and the tapes of her flounced skirts were easy enough to unfasten on her own.

Stripped to her petticoats, chemise, and corset, she crossed the floor to her wardrobe and withdrew a plain cotton day dress. She was just stepping into the skirts when a knock sounded at the door.

Winnifred poked her blond head inside. "May I come in?"

"If you must." Beryl buttoned her skirts at her waist and slipped her arms into the soft sleeves of her bodice. It was an old garment, a faded green print, something she'd often worn in the months before Aunt Hortensia had whisked her away to Paris.

Winnifred came to lean against the end of Beryl's bed. She gave Ernest a distracted scratch. "Do you really intend to go back to the church?"

"I believe I must. Unless you have a better idea?"

"Let me go in your place."

Beryl's fingers stilled on the hooks of her bodice. She gave her sister a puzzled look. "Whatever for?"

"To clean up after Ernest. I can dispose of the greenery and sponge away any leftover mess."

"Why on earth would you want to do that? He's my responsibility."

"I'll happily do it, if...if you'll do something for me in exchange."

Beryl finished fastening her bodice. "This doesn't have anything to do with your argument with Henry, does it?"

"I want you to speak with him."

"About what?" Beryl smoothed her skirts before turning to face her sister. The look on Winnifred's face brought her up short. She was nearly as pale as Mama had been in the carriage. "What is it, dearest?" Beryl went to her and took her hand. "What's happened to upset you so?"

"I'm not upset," Winnifred said. "I'm furious."

"Come. Sit with me." Beryl drew her sister down next to her on the edge of the mattress. The heavy velvet curtains of her four-poster bed cast a shadow over the pair of them, giving a sense of privacy. "Tell me what Henry's done to make you so angry."

"He's an autocratic, overbearing blockhead," Winnifred answered with unexpected heat. "I've been working on him for months, trying to endear myself to him so that he would continue to allow me to ride Vesper. I'd hoped that, one day, he might—" She stopped herself. "But that doesn't matter anymore. It was a stupid dream. I can see that now."

"What? Tell me."

"I had a ridiculous idea that, once the two of you were married, Sir Henry might find it within himself to make me a gift of Vesper."

"Oh, my dear."

"I said it was ridiculous. He's no more likely to give me a horse than he is to do anything out of the goodness of his heart. Indeed, I don't believe he has one."

"Winnie, really. You mustn't say such things."

"What else am I to think? Nothing I've done to sweeten him has made any difference. Not the flowers I've brought or the pleasant conversation I've made with him. I may as well have been conversing with a fence post."

"What's prompted all this?"

Winnifred's mouth trembled. "Yesterday when I went to Rivenhall Park for my ride, the groom said Vesper had been taken out already by Sir Henry. I thought it strange. He usually rides that bay gelding of his. But I wasn't too troubled by it. I assumed he'd forgotten that I'm accustomed to riding Vesper at that time of day. He's been so distracted by business of late. And with your marriage approaching…" She gave a bitter laugh. "You see, even then, I was disposed to give him the benefit of the doubt. But after what he said at church…"

Beryl slipped her arm around Winnifred's shoulders. She stroked her hand up and down her sister's silk-clad arm.

"Vesper should be mine, Beryl." Tears glistened in Winnifred's eyes. "You may think me fanciful, but a rider knows when she's met the horse that was meant for her. We're perfectly suited. And he likes me above anyone. And now Sir Henry says that I can't ride him anymore, simply because I was unseated one dratted time."

Beryl drew back to look at her. She couldn't recall the last time her sister had taken a tumble. "When did this happen?"

"Last week. The morning your wedding dress arrived from Paris. I was riding past Malvern's Emporium, looking at their new window display, when Mrs. Doolittle and her curricle came out of nowhere. Vesper bolted, and I lost my seat. He stopped directly, the silly creature—you never saw a horse look so shamefaced. And I wasn't hurt at all, only a little rumpled. But the groom must have told Sir Henry. If he didn't, then Mrs. Doolittle surely would have. And now I'm barred from riding Vesper ever again."

"Is that what Henry told you?"

"That's not the worst of it. He says... He says he's sending Vesper to the sales in London. That he'll be gone by next week. Sold to the highest bidder."

"Oh, Winnie. I *am* sorry."

"I don't want you to be sorry. I want you to persuade him not to do it. I know he'll listen to you. He must. For if you can't make him change his mind, I don't know what I shall do."

Beryl held her sister close. "Very well. I shall speak with him. But you must pull yourself together. And, I'm afraid, you'll have to look after Ernest while I'm gone. He's not reliable enough yet to visit the Park."

"Gladly."

"It's settled then." She gave Winnifred one last squeeze before rising from the bed to finish dressing. "You'd best change into something more suitable. And do perk up, Winnie. It's not like you to admit defeat so easily."

"I'm not defeated," Winnifred grumbled. "Not yet anyway."

Henry stood from his desk as Mrs. Guthrie showed Beryl into the library at Rivenhall Park. A faint flicker of irritation crossed his face. It was gone as quickly as it came. "Miss Burnham. This is an unexpected pleasure."

Her spirits sank a little. She'd interrupted his work again. It wasn't a very auspicious beginning. "I trust I'm not disturbing you?"

"No, indeed." He addressed the housekeeper. "Tea, Mrs. Guthrie."

"Yes, sir." Mrs. Guthrie dropped a curtsy before exiting the library. She left the door open behind her.

Henry crossed the thick red and gold carpet to take Beryl's hand. "You came alone?"

"I did." She slid her hand from his grasp before he could raise it to his lips. It didn't feel right to let him press his customary kiss to her knuckles. Not after what had happened today between her and Mark. "You think it unwise?"

"We're not married yet."

Yet.

"No," she said, "but we soon will be." And then this would be her home. Henry would be her husband.

The prospect left her strangely chilled.

She turned and walked to the window. The heavy curtains were opened, revealing a pleasant view of the rolling lawn leading down to the stables. It recollected her to her task. "Winnifred was rather upset after church this morning."

"Ah. I see. You've come on her behalf." Henry came to stand beside Beryl at the window. "I owe you and your mother an apology. I should never have permitted your sister to ride that horse in the first place. I might have known she'd become attached to him."

"She *is* attached. Desperately so. She feels he was made for her."

"He's a horse, Beryl. An unreliable one at that."

"Not to her."

"As that may be, I'll not have her injured on his account."

"She wasn't injured."

"Not this time she wasn't."

Beryl's lips compressed. It was plain that Henry had already made up his mind. She knew he was unlikely to be moved by any of her arguments. "Must you sell him?"

"It seems the kindest course. I'd have thought you of all people would agree with me."

She leaned back against the window sill. "Kind? How so?"

"Because keeping him here and forbidding her to ride him will cause more misery for the girl than simply getting rid of him altogether. Once he's gone, she'll soon forget—"

"She won't."

"You must trust my judgment on this."

"And you must respect mine," Beryl said with a trifle more starch than was her habit. "I know my sister."

Henry gave her a long look. "She's distressed you."

"She hasn't—"

"Pity she didn't consider your feelings before enlisting you to come to her aid." Setting a hand at Beryl's back, he guided her to the overstuffed library sofa. "It will do her good to find out what it's like not to get what she wants."

Beryl reluctantly took a seat, her back ramrod straight against one of the sofa's decorative silk-fringed pillows. "You're very hard. Winnifred knows precisely what it's like. She's had to go without ever since my father died, just as my mother and I have done. We none of us are spoiled or overindulged."

Henry remained standing, looming over her in that overbearing way of his. "I don't class the sacrifices you've made with those made by your sister."

"What sacrifices? I've given up nothing I want in the name of economy. While Winnifred has been forced to go without a London season, without a fashionable wardrobe, and now without a riding horse."

"I'll still permit her to ride. There's a mare in my stables that's perfectly suitable for a lady."

"My sister is an excellent rider, Henry. Better than any man. She won't be satisfied with a horse that's lame in all four legs. Besides, it's Vesper who has captured her heart. She's his perfect match."

"Have you ever even seen the pair of them together? He's too big for her, and far too strong. I was a fool to ever permit her to ride him. No. My mind is made up. He goes to the sales this Friday. I've already made the arrangements."

Beryl opened her mouth to object, but Henry forestalled her.

"I'll hear no more on the subject," he said.

She doubted whether he'd heard her at all. Was he so completely unwilling to listen? So utterly opposed to changing his mind? "You won't do it?" she asked. "Not even as a particular favor to me?"

His expression tightened. "This isn't like you."

"To advocate for my sister? Indeed, it is the very essence of me."

"You're becoming overwrought."

Her temper flared quite out of proportion to the circumstances. "And you're becoming unreasonable."

A cough sounded at the door. "Tea, sir." Mrs. Guthrie entered, eyeing the pair of them warily. "Shall I put it here?"

"Yes," Henry said brusquely. "Thank you, Mrs. Guthrie."

Beryl was silent while the housekeeper arranged the tea tray on the low mahogany table in front of the sofa.

"Anything else, sir?" Mrs. Guthrie asked.

"That will be all," Henry said. As the housekeeper exited the room, he added: "Be so good as to close the door behind you."

"Yes, sir." Mrs. Guthrie drew the library door shut with a resounding click.

Beryl's hand froze on the handle of the silver teapot. She looked up at Henry with thinly veiled apprehension. It wasn't his habit to flout propriety.

"We require a moment of privacy," he said.

"That sounds ominous." She resumed pouring their tea, amazed that her hand was so steady. "What is it that you wish to say to me?"

"Only that I'd hoped that when you returned from Paris you would be yourself again. That you would have put all of this nonsense behind you."

Her gaze jerked to his. The teapot clattered as she returned it to the tray. It was a miracle she didn't drop it entirely. "What nonsense?"

Henry sank down into the leather-upholstered armchair across from her. "You've been unsettled. I had reason to believe it was only a temporary condition. That Paris would have remedied it. But it hasn't improved, has it? This tendency you have to—"

"To what?"

"To become emotional."

She stared at him, at a complete loss for words.

"You needn't bother denying it. I had the truth of your condition from Mr. Cooper not long after you left for Paris."

"You what?" she asked faintly.

"He called on me here at the Park last autumn. He told me all."

Her mouth went dry. She couldn't believe it. Surely, she must have misunderstood him somehow. "Do you mean that… you knew? All this time?"

"Naturally."

A wave of nausea threatened to overpower her. Beryl sat back against the sofa cushion, willing it to pass. "But you never…"

He'd never asked after her. Had never made an effort to comfort her.

"You never let on," she said.

"There was little point. Mr. Cooper informed me that, in such cases, it was best to ignore the behavior. To indulge your megrims would only have prolonged the episode."

"Megrims? Is that what you believe was wrong with me?"

"It's what I think, yes. Not what Cooper said. He viewed your condition with a medical eye." Henry ran his fingers through his hair. The gesture reminded Beryl so much of Mark that she had to avert her gaze. "His suggestions for treatment were severe, and I felt, quite unnecessary given your general demeanor. You'd always been sensible enough until then."

Sensible.

Which meant that he believed her sadness—her melancholy—was merely a result of being silly and self-indulgent. It was the very thing she'd feared all along.

"Sense has nothing to do with it," she managed to say. "It's an affliction, like any illness."

"Not according to the doctors."

She gave him a horrified look. "You've consulted others?"

"Not yet, but I've read some of the literature that Cooper provided."

"Mr. Cooper is an unfeeling bully." Beryl's voice rose in long-suppressed hurt and indignation. "How could you listen to him? Why didn't you—"

"What could I have done?" Henry demanded sharply. "Jack had just perished in Bhutan. Did you expect that I would set aside my grief for a much-loved brother in order to cheer your unaccountably low spirits? You who have everything any lady should want—health, beauty, intelligence, and, I flatter myself to add, a rather enviable fiancé?"

She felt the blood drain from her face. So this was what he thought of her? This was how he truly felt about her having left for Paris last year? "I know I let you down. For that I can only beg your pardon. But I would ask that you try to understand—"

"Let me down? You failed the first test as my future wife. It was a moment that required the very best of you. That you be that lady of quiet dignity I'd so come to admire. Instead, you were content to disappear, leaving me to deal with Jack's death on my own. Not to mention the gossip that ensued after your departure."

She blinked rapidly against the threat of tears. Henry had never spoken to her so harshly. Not in all the years she'd known him. "I know that. But it wasn't done on purpose. I would never—"

"Listen to me." Henry leaned forward in his seat. She expected him to take her hand, to offer some variety of civilized reassurance, but he made no move to touch her. "From the moment our betrothal was announced, you became an extension of my good name. Your conduct reflects on me. I know you will think me hard and unfeeling, but I've worked too long to redeem the Rivenhall name to have it damaged."

His words both hurt and shamed her. And yet…she understood. She'd seen the toll it had taken on Henry to restore his family's fortunes. Knew what it must have cost him to face the gossip alone. "I'm sorry. I won't fail you again."

"No. You won't. I'll see to that." Henry's face was set with unwavering resolve. "My father did enough harm indulging his weaknesses. I'll not permit you to do the same. These low spirits of yours, we shall exorcise them. Once we've married, you will see how soon they dissipate."

She felt the unholy urge to laugh—or to weep. She didn't know which. Thank heaven she was able to suppress it. Such behavior would hardly bolster Henry's confidence in her. "You sound very sure of yourself."

"I am. Mr. Cooper had suggestions."

Her face fell. Not Mr. Cooper again. It seemed the man and his odious medical opinions would haunt her to her grave. "Surely you don't countenance—"

"Yes, yes, I know what you think of the fellow. Any female might feel the same given the circumstances. But you cannot discount his medical opinion."

"I do discount it, most strenuously."

"Some of what he recommended was harsh, I grant you. However, he did have one suggestion that struck me as being eminently sensible." Henry picked up his teacup. "I hope we might discuss it further after we're married."

After they were married? She could no longer imagine it. All she wanted was to leave this place. To run all the way back to her bedroom at the Grange, and to the illusion of security that it gave her.

Good lord. To think, she'd come here to argue over the fate of a horse!

"I've already heard his suggestions," she said, "as has my mother, and none of them deserve consideration."

"You won't have heard this one." Henry paused before adding, "It's of a delicate nature."

She steeled herself for the worst. "What is it? What did he suggest?"

Henry sipped his tea in silence.

Beryl had never been so frustrated with a person in her life. "Really, Henry. If you think I'm going to wait until we're married to find out, you must be dreaming."

"This willfulness is unbecoming."

"I daresay it is. Nevertheless, I must demand that you tell me now. It's my own health we're speaking of, not some aspect of your personal business."

Henry's mouth tightened. "Very well. If you insist." He lowered his teacup back to its saucer. "Cooper gave me to understand that your spirits would settle once I got you with child."

A blazing heat crept into Beryl's face. "He *said* that?"

The very thought of it shocked her already tattered senses. And yet Henry could reference the condition with such calm matter-of-factness! As if the getting of that child wouldn't entail the greatest intimacy of her life.

Intimacy with *him*.

"He did, yes," Henry said. "And I tend to agree with him. Children will give you something to occupy yourself. You'll be too busy with them to pander to your low spirits."

"Children," she repeated. "You speak of more than one."

"Naturally," he said. "If we're blessed in that regard."

She wondered how many blessings he had in mind. A half dozen? More? The prospect nearly had her racing from the room.

What lady desired to be rushed into childbed? It was fraught with risk. One was always hearing stories of women dying or being made an invalid from the experience.

And what about the intimacy that came before? The necessary intimacy? All this talk of children, and yet she'd never properly considered that aspect of her impending marriage. Never truly contemplated the reality of sharing Henry's bed. If she'd thought of it at all, it was only in terms of a duty. Something to be got through. Not unpleasant, but certainly not enjoyable. Mama had alluded to that much.

Beryl hadn't questioned her further. And she certainly hadn't interrogated her own feelings on the matter. Not until now, sitting across from her soon-to-be husband. A man who'd known about her melancholy all along. Who was mapping out the course of her married life with the same ruthless efficiency he used to determine the next season's plantings on his estate.

She brought a hand to her temple, feeling the beginnings of a headache. "And these children are going to cure me?"

"You sound skeptical. But I suspect that once you're a mother—"

"What if they don't? What if I get worse instead of better? Am I to simply keep having children until I expire from—"

"Beryl." His voice held a note of warning.

"It's a ridiculous solution," she said. "It's… It's not what I want."

"Perhaps not, but you don't understand human biology." He gave her a tight smile. "That's why we employ doctors. It's their job to tell us what's best for our health. We'd be wise to take their advice."

Chapter Nine

Mark stood silent in the corner of Mrs. Priddy's darkened kitchen as Dr. Black bandaged her broken arm. That injury, at least, could be set and mended. Her black eye and swollen lip were another matter.

Bruised and battered, the woman's work-worn face was almost unrecognizable. She was seated in a wooden chair at a table still cluttered with breakfast leavings—half-eaten bowls of congealed porridge and cold mugs of tea. "It's the drink, Dr. Black. My husband wouldn't hurt me otherwise."

Black was hearing none of it. His mouth had been set in a grim frown from the moment he'd entered the cottage and seen Mrs. Priddy's condition. "He chooses to drink."

"Not much choice in it. He can't resist the temptation of the bottle."

"It doesn't excuse what he's done to you," Black said.

Mrs. Priddy winced as the doctor carefully maneuvered her arm. "His life's not been easy, my Bert. He's had his share of disappointments."

Mark sank to his haunches beside her chair, bringing their faces level. "Do you know where he's gone?"

She averted her gaze. "He didn't say. To town, I expect."

Mark didn't believe her. But there was no point in pressing the matter. Not in her current condition. He'd have to find Bert Priddy on his own.

Black tied off the bandage. "You'll need to refrain from getting it wet."

"But I must do, sir," she said. "I've got yesterday's laundry to finish, and more bags of it coming tomorrow."

"No laundry." Black snapped shut his medical bag. "No exertion of any kind, not for several days."

Mrs. Priddy gave Mark a look of distress. "I've got to work, Mr. Rivenhall. That laundry is what keeps food in my children's bellies."

Mark set a hand on her uninjured arm. "Don't distress yourself. I'll find someone to assist you until you've recovered."

"Is it too much to expect that her husband might support them?" Black asked under his breath as he and Mark exited the cottage.

It was a beautiful day in Shepton Worthy, the summer wind whispering gently through the late-blooming blossoms on the trees. One would never guess at the unpleasantness that lurked inside some of the neat little thatched cottages that lined the lane.

"Bert Priddy used to be a day laborer," Mark said. "I'd sometimes see him in the fields at Rivenhall Park. But that was long ago. Long before his children were born and he turned to the bottle."

"Has he ever done this before?"

"Not that she's been willing to admit."

Black bent his head. A muscle twitched in his jaw. "He might have killed her."

Mark was only too aware. "Something must be done, of course."

"Such as?"

"I'll speak to her husband if I can find him—though I don't expect he'll show his face around here anytime soon." Mark was both angered and frustrated by the situation. Despite his best efforts, there was only so much he could achieve when the violence that occurred was between husband and wife. "I suppose, all else failing, I could mention the matter to my brother."

"Is Sir Henry likely to intervene?"

"I doubt it. He doesn't like to meddle in the lives of his tenants, even for the good. He'll usually only exert himself if a law was broken."

"It should be a crime," Black said.

"Indeed." But it wasn't. Bert Priddy wouldn't suffer any punishment for beating his wife. Not unless some well-meaning gentleman got it into his head to teach the man a lesson. At the moment, Mark felt rather like doing the job himself.

"The man should be ostracized from polite society," Black said. "Though I don't suppose he will be. Not here. People like Mrs. Priddy are next door to invisible in this godforsaken village."

"Shepton Worthy isn't unique in that regard."

"No. It's worse." Black heaved a weary sigh. "I sometimes wonder if I wouldn't do better somewhere else. A village less committed to outward appearances."

Mark gave a short laugh. There was nothing of humor in it. "If you find such a place, do let me know."

"You're not considering moving to another parish?"

"I might be."

Black shot him a sharp glance. "By choice?"

"Not mine."

"Your brother's?"

Mark hesitated. It went against the grain to discuss his relationship with Henry, especially as it related to Beryl. But Simon Black had become a friend. There was no use dissembling. "He's indicated that, when Venable retires, he may grant the living to someone else."

Black was quiet for a long moment. "Perhaps it's for the best."

"Perhaps," Mark said. That didn't prevent him from feeling hollow inside at the prospect. As if all the happiness and optimism had been drained from his life.

"As a point of interest, my father has the living available on his estate. He mentioned it in his last letter. I daresay he's still holding out hope that, one day, I might give up medicine and return to the church." Black went silent again before offering, "I can put in a word, if you like."

"Dorset, isn't it?" If Mark remembered, the Earl of Harbury's estate was located somewhere near Wimborne. "That's not too far from here."

"Far enough," Black said. "It may be just the thing for you."

Mark bent his head. He couldn't imagine a life without the hope of seeing Beryl each day. Without the joy of making her smile. A growing sadness welled within him. "Very well," he replied. "If you would make inquiries, I'd be obliged to you."

He walked with Black up the lane and onto the main street. Black's surgery was situated on the corner, a wooden shingle over the door proclaiming his name and profession. There Mark took his leave. He was needed back at the church. The ladies' committee was finishing preparations for the fete and he'd promised Mrs. Malvern he would assist with setting up some of the stalls on the green.

It would mean seeing Beryl again.

Mark both longed for and dreaded the moment.

He hadn't crossed paths with her since their ill-fated encounter outside the church. That hadn't stopped him from replaying their kiss over and over in his mind. From meditating on the softness of her lips and the feeling of her body pressed so intimately to his.

Such memories were bittersweet. They warred with less pleasant recollections. The way she'd looked when she'd broken away from him—shocked, stricken. The way her voice had trembled.

"*I've ruined everything,*" she'd said.

Mark hated to think of it. Doing so only caused him to feel hurt and embarrassment, and a sense of loss so keen he could focus on nothing else.

Back at the vicarage, he looked in on a sleeping Mr. Venable before walking down to the village green. The ladies were already gathered there, along with several of the village men they'd pressed into service.

"What do you think, Mr. Rivenhall?" Mrs. Malvern asked. She was wearing a paint-stained apron over her fashionable day dress. "Not too shabby for a half day's work, if I do say so myself."

Wooden stalls were arrayed over the green. Those that were finished had received a coat of white paint. Others were still under construction. Men shouted back and forth to each other as they sawed and hammered.

"You've made great progress," Mark said.

"Owing to our brawny volunteers. We mean to thank them by feeding them. Mrs. Doolittle and Mrs. White should be back any moment with hampers of sandwiches and lemonade. No doubt the men would prefer cold beer, but you know how some of our ladies feel about strong drink."

Mark's gaze drifted over the green. "Is Miss Burnham not here?"

"Indeed not. I believe she's unwell. Her mother sent a note round to that effect this morning. Such a pity, too, for Miss Burnham was going to bring her wedding dress to the Emporium this afternoon. My husband is anxious to examine the design." Mrs. Malvern looked up at him. "You don't think it's anything serious?"

What Mark thought was that he was an unpardonable idiot.

He'd been too caught up in worrying over his own hurt feelings—his own injured pride—to consider what that kiss must have meant to Beryl. She was bound to view it in the most negative terms. To be feeling even more at sea. As if she'd done something unforgivable.

Had he been thinking clearly, he'd have mustered the nerve to call on her the very same day. Instead, he'd left her alone, to languish in guilt and self-recrimination.

It wouldn't do.

He looked back toward the road, wishing that he'd had the forethought to have brought the gig. It was over a mile's walk to the Grange.

"Mr. Rivenhall?" Mrs. Malvern asked. "Are you all right?"

"Yes. Quite." He forced a smile, certain it must look more like a grimace. "Forgive me. There's a matter I must attend to. If you'll excuse me?"

"By all means. We have volunteers enough for today."

Mark departed the green without looking back. He'd walked to the Grange countless times over the years, but never before with such haste. Arriving at the door, he was greeted by the housekeeper, Mrs. Witherspoon, who showed him into the drawing room.

He was too anxious to sit down. He paced from the marble fireplace to the velvet-draped windows and back again, his hands clasped at his back.

When at last the drawing room door opened, he came to an abrupt halt, his pulse quickening with expectation. But it wasn't Beryl who entered. It was her mother.

An expression of relief came over Mrs. Burnham's face at the sight of him. "Mr. Rivenhall. I was just deliberating on whether or not to summon you. Imagine my surprise when Mrs. Witherspoon informed me that you were already here."

Mark stepped forward. "You were going to send for me? Why?"

"It was either you or Dr. Black. My daughter's been quite unwell, you see." Mrs. Burnham took a seat, motioning for him to do the same. "I've been at sixes and sevens all morning."

He sat down across from her on the very edge of a petit-point armchair. "I beg your pardon, ma'am. I must ask…

Is Miss Burnham's illness of a similar nature to that which plagued her last year?"

"Mr. Venable spoke to you? Good heavens. Beryl feared he might. Oh, but I did assure her—"

"It wasn't Venable. It was Miss Burnham herself. If she's unwell, I should dearly like to see her. It's why I've come. Unless, of course, it's a medical matter, in which case—"

"I don't know that it *is* a medical matter," Mrs. Burnham said. "It's precisely why I've been fretting so, trying to decide whether to summon a clergyman or a physician."

"Has Miss Burnham asked for a doctor?"

"No indeed. She never would. And I don't expect she'd thank me for summoning one. She had a rather difficult experience with Mr. Cooper." Mrs. Burnham's brow puckered. "I'd thought she was doing better. She's been so looking forward to the fete, and to her wedding to Sir Henry. Her wedding dress came last week, did she tell you? All the way from Paris. I confess, I wept when I saw her in it. How any young lady could be glum in such circumstances, I don't know. But when she returned from the Park—"

"She visited Rivenhall Park?" Mark's blood went cold. "When?"

"On Sunday. Not long after we came home from church. She was gone only a short while. When she returned, she had a few words with Winnifred and then retired to her room. She's been quiet and withdrawn ever since. And it's worsening by the day. Last night, I couldn't even persuade her to join us for dinner." Mrs. Burnham gave him a bleak look. "I ask you, sir, what has my daughter to be unhappy about? She has everything a young lady could want, and is poised to have even more."

Mark could barely bring himself to answer. His chest was tight with anxiety. "I don't believe her unhappiness has anything to do with that."

"No. No, I don't suppose it does." Mrs. Burnham stared at the fireplace, briefly losing herself in thought.

"May I see her?" Mark asked.

"Yes, I think you'd better." She rose from her seat. "A clergyman might succeed where a mother has failed."

He accompanied her upstairs, following her to a wood-paneled door at the end of a dimly lit hallway. Motioning for him to wait, she rapped once before slipping inside. A long minute passed before she emerged.

"You may go in," she said, holding the door wide.

Mark had never been inside Beryl's bedroom before. A four-poster bed stood at its center, green velvet hangings tied back to reveal a neatly folded coverlet and bolster. There was a dressing table, wardrobe, and washstand. A comfortable chair poised by the fireplace.

It wasn't so very different from other ladies' bedrooms he'd visited in the course of his parish duties. And yet…

The details were distinctly *her*.

A patchwork quilt lay folded at the end of her bed, a colorful ceramic pitcher sat upon the washstand, and a needlepoint pillow was propped in the chair. Delicate crystal bottles and a set of silver-plated hairbrushes graced the surface of her dressing table, and in front of the fireplace stood an artfully painted screen adorned with images of wildflowers.

Her whitework embroidery must be here, as well. He sensed it, somewhere beneath the surface, ornamenting the edge of a linen bedsheet or the hem of a petticoat folded within the wardrobe. Those tiny embroidered damselflies and butterflies. Her secret self, hidden from view.

The whole of the room was alluringly feminine, bright with sunlight and whispering with the faint fragrance of elderflower. And there, curled in the cushioned window seat, a cashmere shawl half draped around her shoulders, was Beryl herself.

Garbed in a plain white muslin day dress, her golden hair caught up in a haphazard knot at her nape, she looked more beautiful than on any other occasion Mark had beheld her.

Beautiful, and exceedingly vulnerable.

There were blue marks under her eyes, and an expression on her face that was both anxious and weary.

He went to her with concern, vaguely conscious of Mrs. Burnham closing the door behind him. She never hesitated to leave the two of them alone. As a curate, he wasn't seen as being a threat to Beryl's reputation.

The irony of that fact didn't escape him.

"May I?" He motioned to the place beside her.

"If you wish."

As he sat down, Ernest stood from Beryl's lap and gave a half-hearted bark. She soothed him with a pet before gently depositing him onto the floor.

Mark smiled. "I'm pleased to see you haven't been entirely alone."

She twined her drooping shawl more firmly about her arms. "Being alone isn't always so bad. Sometimes I prefer it."

"Would you rather I'd not come?"

"No. I'm glad to see you."

One wouldn't know it by her demeanor. There was a weight of sadness in her gaze. A dull, lost look. As if the whole of her world had turned inward.

He tried again. "Your mother said you went to the Park after church on Sunday."

She gazed out the window. The Grange's rosebushes were in full bloom below, bloodred roses vying for attention with those of white, yellow, and the palest porcelain pink.

He wondered if she even saw them. She seemed very far away. "Did you speak with Henry?"

"Yes."

"And did you…" He hesitated, a creeping warmth rising under his cravat. "Did you tell him that I kissed you?"

At last she looked at him. Her blue-green eyes were startlingly direct. "Is that what you think happened?"

"I don't know what to think. I only know that you were upset when we parted. That you feared you'd damaged your relationship with Henry. You were quite distraught at the possibility."

"I never was."

"You were," he assured her. "I distinctly recall it. You said that you'd ruined everything."

Understanding registered in Beryl's face. "I wasn't talking about Henry. I was talking about us."

Us.

A simple word, but in that instant, it was as powerful as a magical incantation. It changed the chemistry of the moment. Altering the very rhythm of Mark's pulse and breath.

He felt something fracture inside of him. Long-held beliefs about who was first and best in her heart. He'd misinterpreted things. Got them all backward. It wasn't Henry she feared losing. It was him. The realization struck his composure a devastating blow.

"Our friendship is more important to me than anything," she said. "I don't know what I'd do if I couldn't see you again."

"There's no chance of that." His voice went gruff. "It would take more than a kiss to ruin things between us."

She didn't look very convinced. "Even if Henry finds out?"

"You didn't tell him?

"Would you mind terribly if I had?"

"No. Not if you felt you needed to." It was the truth. The day they'd kissed, he'd said that Henry need never know. That nothing could be achieved by telling him. Mark still believed that, but he would never expect Beryl to betray her own conscience.

"I didn't," she said. "Not yet anyway."

"Then why did you go to the Park on Sunday?" he asked. "If not to tell Henry, then—"

"I went to talk to him about my sister. About that horse she loves so much."

"Vesper?"

"Winnifred thought I could persuade Henry not to sell him. But he won't relent. Not even for my sake."

Mark wasn't surprised. Once set on a course, Henry could rarely be moved. "I'm sorry to hear it."

"It's Winnifred who deserves your pity, not me. You should have seen the look on her face when I told her. She was crushed."

"And this is why you've taken to your room?"

"That's not the reason." Beryl looked out the window again. Her face was pale. "Henry knows about me."

Mark went still. "What about you?"

"Everything. He knows what happened with the sleeping powder. Why I went to Paris last year with Aunt Hortensia. He's known all along. About my melancholy. All of it."

Mark was thunderstruck. "How?"

"Mr. Cooper told him shortly after I left. And Henry—" Her voice cracked. "He's so dreadfully disappointed in me."

"The devil he is."

"He says I failed the first test as his future wife. And he's right. I've failed at everything. I've been selfish and self-indulgent. It's past time I grew up."

Mark's temper rose. How dared he. How *dared* he. "He said this to you?"

"It's nothing I haven't heard before."

"From whom? Not me. Not your mother. Henry has no right—"

"Mr. Cooper told him so. It's what all doctors believe."

"They don't, I promise you."

"Indeed, they do." Beryl rose from her seat. "Here. I'll show you." She crossed the room to her bed, sinking down on the floor beside it in a pool of white skirts and petticoats. Sliding her hand underneath the mattress, she withdrew something that looked like a magazine.

Resuming her seat, she opened it on a folded page. "It's here, plain as day."

Mark frowned. "What is that?"

"A copy of the *Provincial Medical and Surgical Gazette*. Mr. Cooper gave it to Mama last year, so that she would know what it was she was dealing with. He meant me. My melancholy." She extended it to him. Her hand shook. "You can read it for yourself."

"Beryl—"

"No," she said. "I want you to."

He reluctantly took it. The article she'd bookmarked was on the subject of acute melancholia, and was purported to have been written by a Fellow of the Royal College of Physicians in London. Mark's gaze moved swiftly over the small typewritten text.

> *Everyone must be struck by the intense self-feeling of the melancholy man. His egotism exceeds even that of the paralytic or maniac. He thinks that everything is centered in him. His superlative misery is a theme on which he loves to descant. His depression is great, but he magnifies it in the recital of his woes.*[1]

Mark had expected a cold denunciation of her feelings, but this was worse, so much worse, than he'd anticipated. He tossed the journal aside in disgust. "This is rubbish."

She picked it up again. "It's confirmed medical opinion."

"Yes, precisely. *Opinion.* It isn't you."

"But there's more." She turned to another folded page. "You can see for yourself."

"Beryl—"

"It says here that the melancholy patient is selfish. That they desire nothing more than coddling at the expense of everyone around them. And that—"

He stilled her hand on the page. "I don't need to see any more."

---

1 Blandford, George Fielding. *Insanity and its Treatment: Lectures on the Treatment, Medical and Legal, of Insane Patients.* Philadelphia: Henry C. Lea, 1871.

She stared down at the medical journal. Her fingers were clenched around it, holding it tight. A shaft of warm sunlight through the window illuminated the right side of her face, leaving the left in shadow.

It occurred to Mark then that she'd always been thus. A part of her shadowed. Hidden from view as surely as she hid her whitework. That vulnerable, hurting side of herself she never dared show to anyone for fear of being judged and found wanting.

But she was showing it to him now. Trusting him above anyone else.

"Let it go," he said gently. "Let me take it away."

Her eyes squeezed shut, her voice quavering. "He told my mother that I must enjoy the attention. Perhaps he was right. I wanted to see you, and now you're here."

"I'll always be here when you need me. I should have come sooner."

"You don't understand. It's not you, it's me. Melancholy makes people manipulative. The journal says—"

"It's rubbish," he said again. His fingers curled gently around hers. "Let it go, sweetheart."

Chapter Ten

The soft endearment fell like a honeyed balm on Beryl's frayed nerves. Mark had never before called her *sweetheart*. She was certain she'd remember if he had. The effect was that dramatic. It warmed her. Soothed her. Made her list closer to him, secretly longing for more of his voice and his touch.

She could scarcely believe that only two days ago he'd kissed her. On her return from church, she'd wondered how she would ever again look him in the eye. How she would ever speak to him normally. And yet, here he was, being her friend. Closer, and somehow dearer, because of that kiss. Because she knew how well the two of them fit together. As if they were made for each other, body and soul.

Slowly, she loosened her grip on the medical journal, permitting him to take it from her. Her heart lurched as she felt it slip away.

He folded it and tucked it behind him, well out of her reach. "Why do you keep such a thing?"

"I don't know." She'd often puzzled over that herself. It was a perverse compulsion. "I suppose it's to make myself face the facts, unpleasant as they are."

"And you reread it? When you're at your most vulnerable?" He looked vaguely appalled. "Why would you torture yourself that way?"

Beryl's mouth trembled. It *was* torture. She was hurt every time she read it, each recitation of the words reopening a wound she'd never fully permitted to heal. "Because I don't want to forget what I can be at my worst. I want to strive to do better."

"By berating yourself with the opinions of men who don't even know you? Who have no idea what a wonderful, giving, extraordinary person you are?"

Tears stung at the back of her eyes. "You don't have to say that."

"It seems to me that someone needs to say it to you, and often." He shot a revolted glance at the discarded medical journal. "If you require a medical opinion, consult with someone, by all means. But let it be a man like Dr. Black. A modern thinker, not some antiquated relic who would have you believing your melancholy is merely the result of vanity and self-indulgence."

She'd never heard Mark speak in such a way. He sounded almost angry. "Are you upset with me?"

"I'm concerned about you. It's Henry I'm upset with. I could throttle him for saying those things to you."

"Yes, well..." She pushed a stray strand of hair back from her face, relieved to see that her fingers were no longer shaking. "He's had to endure quite a bit on my account. The gossip and the—"

"He's your betrothed. The man who loves you. It should be his privilege to endure such things on your behalf."

"You're wrong."

"Indeed, I'm not. If I were your—" He stopped himself. The strong column of his throat convulsed on a swallow. "What I mean to say is that any gentleman worth the name would be honored to protect you. He wouldn't blame you. And he certainly wouldn't upset you to the point that—"

"Not about that." Embarrassment coiled tight in her breast. "You're wrong about Henry loving me."

Mark stared at her.

Heat seeped into her cheeks. "He doesn't. Not in the way you mean." She twined her fingers into her shawl, feeling a sudden surge of self-consciousness. "He never has done."

"But the two of you…" Mark faltered. "I thought—"

"I was merely close at hand. There are no other ladies near to his rank in the village. None that would suit him. And Henry's never been the sort to venture farther. Not with Rivenhall Park to think of. He's consumed by thoughts of his estate. Romance has always been a secondary concern."

"You make it sound as though his proposing to you was a matter of convenience."

"Perhaps it was, for him."

"And yet I know for a fact that he admires you greatly."

"Oh yes, he admires me. Or rather, he did, until Mr. Cooper told him about my episodes of melancholy."

Mark searched her face. His blue eyes were dark with some unfathomable emotion. "Do you love him?"

She looked back out the window. Mama was down below, her apron firmly in place, snipping away the dead heads of her roses.

"Beryl?"

"No," she said quietly. "I don't love Henry."

Mark stood abruptly from the window seat. He strode to the bed and back again in an agitated state, coming to halt in front of her. "Why on earth did you agree to marry him?"

"Many people marry who aren't in love. It's exceedingly common."

"But you... You're not common. You're..." He raked a hand through his hair. "You deserve happiness. To be with someone who worships the ground you tread on."

"I have no desire to be worshiped."

"You know what I mean. Someone who'll care for you. Value you. Who'll respect your tender feelings, not crush them into dust." His hand fell back to his side. "If Henry feels that your episode of melancholy last year was a failure as his future wife, how do you imagine he'll feel when the next episode occurs? And the next?"

Beryl knew exactly how Henry would feel. "He'll be disappointed in me, naturally. I tried to tell him so. But he didn't credit my opinion on the matter. He believes there's a cure for my melancholy. He says that..."

Mark's brows snapped together. "What?"

She could barely bring herself to repeat it. Such things weren't discussed. Certainly not in mixed company. "He says that my mood will settle once he gets me with child."

A flush of color rose above the line of Mark's cravat. "Did he, by God."

"Mr. Cooper put the idea in his head. He told him that children help to distract a lady from her low spirits, and that, in many cases, they can effect a permanent cure."

"There is no cure," Mark said. "Not a legitimate one. There's naught available but quackery and experimental treatments. As for children..." An odd expression passed over his face. "I suppose the reasoning is that you'd be too busy with them to give a thought to your troubles?"

"Something like that."

"It's ludicrous."

"That's what I said. But Henry——" She broke off as realization sank in. "How is it that you know so much about cures and treatments?" Her gaze turned accusing. "You didn't discuss my condition with Dr. Black?"

"I did," he admitted. "But only in the abstract."

She drew back. "What did you tell him?"

"Nothing about you." Mark stepped forward, closing the lost distance between them. His broad shoulder came to rest against the window frame. "I promise. We spoke in general terms."

"And he says there's nothing that can be done?" She'd known that already. Known it and accepted it. The fact nevertheless caused a dull pain in her heart.

"He recommends the very things you've already done by instinct. Healthy occupation. Sunlight and fresh air. Activities to take you out of yourself."

"And when the melancholy strikes in spite of all that? Because it will. There's no way to keep it entirely at bay."

Mark came closer, bunching the skirts of her day dress with his legs. "I have my own opinions on the subject."

Her pulse jumped. She feared his censure more than anyone's. "You think I should behave differently?"

"What I think—what I sincerely believe—is that you need to surround yourself with people who love and support you unconditionally. Who'll show compassion during your dark moments, not criticize and shame you for something over which you have no control."

She doubted such people existed. Not everyone in her life was as harsh on the subject as Henry, but even Mama had plainly been pushed to her limits by Beryl's low spirits. If her mother couldn't show unconditional support during such times, how could Beryl expect such love and understanding from a man?

A small needful part of her wanted to ask Mark how he would have behaved in Henry's place. If he would have exhibited such patience and understanding.

But she already knew the answer.

That day by the riverbank, Mark had shown her just how compassionate he could be. He'd sat with her and listened to her. Had read to her, and rubbed her back so very gently.

"I want you to leave this burden with me for a day or two," he'd said.

She'd thought him altogether wrongheaded. And then…

And then, he'd given her a journal. He'd given her Ernest.

"How can you feel unloved," he'd asked, *"when there's someone with you who loves you so devotedly?"*

Ernest was presently curled up on the carpet, occasionally opening one eye to assure himself of her safety.

And Mark was here.

He'd come to her, despite the discomfort he must feel after their kiss. He'd come to make sure she was all right, bringing no judgments or burden of guilt. Expecting nothing in return.

Her heartbeat accelerated, swift as a hummingbird's. "May I ask you something?"

"Whatever you'd like."

"Sunday, outside the church…you said what happened between us didn't mean anything." Her face burned with a blush that was almost painful. "Was that true?"

He looked steadily back at her. A taut silence stretched between them. "No. It wasn't," he said at last. "Quite the reverse."

She could think of nothing else to say. Could only look at him, wondering how in the world she'd ever been so blind.

"It's not ideal, I know," he said. "This love I have for you. Have always had." He gave a rueful grimace. "When you left for Paris, I prayed that God would take it from me. That I could be rid of it once and for all."

Love, he'd said. Not affection or admiration. Not merely friendship.

Love.

Her head was spinning. "He didn't?" she asked faintly.

"No. He didn't. And I've come to understand why." His voice deepened. "It's because knowing you—being your friend—has been the blessing of my life."

She bowed her head. "Oh, Mark." Emotion dammed up in her chest. "You'll make me cry."

His fingers brushed her cheek. A tender caress with the back of his knuckles. Warm and fleeting. "Please don't. I wouldn't have confessed it except…I suspect you'd rather have the truth from me, inconvenient as it is."

"Why did you never say anything?"

"What could I have said? You've always belonged to my brother."

She blinked away the threat of tears. "I don't belong to anyone. But you're right. We shouldn't speak of this. I'm not free."

Not yet.

A spark lit within her. Good gracious. Was it even possible at this stage? To extricate herself from this tangle?

The prospect both thrilled and terrified her.

"I know that," Mark said. "Which is why I must apologize for what happened between us on Sunday. For feeling as I do. We neither of us want to harm our friendship—or to hurt Henry." He managed a tight smile. "Insufferable tyrant that he is."

Beryl had the sense that he'd misunderstood her somehow, but before she could explain herself, her attention was caught by a movement outside the window. A large gray horse passed swiftly through the rose garden below. She looked out in time to see its tail end disappear from view.

"Is that what I think it was?" Mark asked.

"I fear it was." She rose hastily from her seat. "Either Henry's relented at last. Or…"

Or her sister had just stolen a horse.

Chapter Eleven

*M*ark stood alongside Beryl inside the Grange's modestly-sized stables. Made of brick, with a wood-shingled roof, they'd been empty for as long as he could remember. Riding horses were an expense that the Burnham family couldn't afford. Instead, the stables served as temporary quarters for Mrs. Sheldrake's carriage horses—and as a convenient trellis for Mrs. Burnham's climbing roses. Buds of pink and red ran up the faded walls and drooped over the green-painted doors.

Vesper's enormous gray head hung out of one of the looseboxes. Winnifred cradled his muzzle in her hand. Ernest gave the skirts of her dirt-streaked blue riding habit an interested sniff.

Beryl swept the little dog up in her arms before he could do any harm.

"Have you taken leave of your senses?" Mrs. Sheldrake demanded of Winnifred. She gesticulated at Vesper. "What you've done is a crime!"

"It would have been a crime to leave him there," Winnifred retorted. "None of Sir Henry's grooms know how to handle him. He won't submit to anyone but me."

"You can't just steal a horse, my dear," Mrs. Burnham said.

"I haven't stolen him. I've *rescued* him." Winnifred flung a defiant glance at Mark. "And I don't care what your brother says about it. I'm not giving him back. Not even if Sir Henry calls in the magistrate."

"My brother *is* the magistrate," Mark reminded her.

"Oh." Winnifred's face fell. She instantly rallied. "Still, he isn't likely to make a scandal out of it, is he? You know how he feels about gossip."

"They hang horse thieves," Mrs. Sheldrake said. "And with good reason. You'll take that creature back at once, and pray Sir Henry doesn't have you brought up on charges."

"Really, Aunt," Beryl chided, adjusting Ernest more comfortably in her arms. "Henry's hardly going to sentence Winnifred to be hanged."

"Exactly." Winnifred stroked the horse's face. "By taking Vesper, I've simply presented him with a fait accompli."

"He won't see it that way," Mark said. "All you'll have achieved is to make him ten times more committed to his course."

Beryl agreed. "I'm sorry, dearest, but Mr. Rivenhall is right. You must take Vesper back."

Winnifred gave Beryl an anguished look. "I won't do it."

"Foolish, headstrong girl." Mrs. Sheldrake turned on her heel, her body stiff with matronly indignation. "I wash my hands of the matter."

Mrs. Burnham made a soft sound of irritation. "And now you've upset your aunt." She strode off after Mrs. Sheldrake, untying her apron as she went.

Mark was left with Beryl and Winnifred.

"I asked her for the money to buy him," Winnifred confessed.

"Aunt Hortensia?" Beryl's brows lifted. "When?"

"Yesterday. Not long after you returned from Rivenhall Park. It seemed the wisest thing to do."

"Oh, Winnie…"

"I don't think it so very out of order to ask if Aunt Hortensia would buy him for me." Winnifred paused. "For us, I mean. His upkeep would be no more than for the field horses."

Mark didn't know about that. Riding horses were notoriously expensive.

"What did she say?" Beryl asked.

"She flat out refused. Indeed, she acted as though I was out of my wits for even thinking she had such a sum to spare. And why shouldn't I have thought so? She took you to Paris for an entire year!"

"That was different," Beryl said.

"Yes," Winnifred shot back. "It was *more* expensive than a horse would be."

"An expense that was Aunt Hortensia's own idea, and marriage the ultimate goal of it. Can't you see, my dear? To her it was a practical matter, not an indulgence. She looked on our stay in Paris—all the things she bought for me—as something of an investment."

Mark regarded Beryl with a pensive frown. The way she spoke of her impending marriage to Henry. As if she not only understood that it was a purely practical matter, void of all emotion, but that she accepted it as such. As if she didn't need more. *Deserve* more.

It troubled him greatly.

"Why did you never say anything?" she'd asked him.

He wondered if it would have made a difference. If knowing how much he loved her would have prompted her to refuse Henry's offer of marriage. To disappoint her family's expectations—to forego wealth and security—and all for what? To be the wife of a humble curate? A man of little wealth and no property.

It was the very reason he'd never said anything. He'd been waiting. Hoping that one day—*some* day—when he was in a position to ask her, she'd still be there, free to accept him.

But that day had never come.

And now, it never would.

"I'm not free," she'd said.

As if he hadn't known that from the moment she'd accepted Henry's proposal. He'd understood then that a part of her was lost to him forever. He still loved her. He couldn't imagine a day when he wouldn't, not even after they were separated by her marriage and his removal to some distant parish.

The kind of love he felt for Beryl Burnham didn't flicker out merely because they didn't see each other. A year apart hadn't managed to extinguish it. He suspected that nothing ever would.

"I wish Aunt Hortensia would make an investment in my happiness," Winnifred said. "Not in my future marriage, but in *me*. In something I love."

"How much is my brother asking for him?" Mark inquired.

"Five hundred pounds," Winnifred said.

"*Five hundred pounds?*" Beryl sucked in a breath. "Surely that's just a number he made up to discourage your interest?"

Winnifred shook her head. "I asked the groom at the Park. Apparently the price is on account of Vesper's bloodlines. As if I cared one jot for who his parents were. But some man will care. Some rich wastrel who'll buy Vesper at the sales in London and run him straight into the ground."

Beryl set Ernest down again. The little dog promptly trotted off to lift his leg on some gardening equipment. "He must know by now that you've taken him."

"Probably." Winnifred pressed her cheek to Vesper's nose. "No doubt he's in a towering fury." A frown worked its way between her brows. "Do you think he'll come after me?"

"I'll speak with him," Mark said. He needed to see Henry anyway to discuss Bert Priddy. He might as well kill two unpleasant birds with one stone.

"No." Beryl placed a staying hand on his arm. "I'll go."

He looked at her. "You needn't—"

"I must." An expression of single-minded intention came over her face. "And I must do it alone."

Aunt Hortensia permitted Beryl to use the carriage for her visit. It was quicker than walking. More convenient, too, as it allowed her to make a brief stop in the village first. "Malvern's Emporium," she told the coachman.

"Right-o, miss."

She sank back in her seat. Her palms were damp, and her stomach quavering. She wondered if she'd quite lost her mind.

But no.

Her nerves notwithstanding, she felt more determined than she had in ages.

And it was all entirely her own idea. No one else knew a thing. Indeed, no one at the Grange had even seen her off. Mama had been too busy tending to Aunt Hortensia, and Winnifred had been occupied looking after Ernest and Vesper. As for Mark, he'd reluctantly taken his leave long before Beryl departed. She'd assured him that his parish duties were more important than a minor domestic quibble.

But it was more than that to her. More than a disagreement about a horse.

A trembling courage built within her. It wasn't a blind courage. She knew very well what the consequences would be. Mama and Aunt Hortensia would be disappointed in her. And there would be gossip—worse than Beryl had endured thus far.

But gossip was a temporary thing. A marriage was forever. The rest of her life, until death would she part. Was it worth avoiding the one by being sentenced to the other?

She didn't think so.

By the time the carriage stopped in front of Malvern's Emporium, her courageous impulse had hardened to a firm resolve. She entered the shop, with its elegant window display of sprigged muslin summer frocks and pastel silk parasols. The bell over the polished wood door tinkled to announce her arrival.

Mr. Malvern looked up from behind the cutting counter. "Miss Burnham! I was hoping you might stop in today."

"I'm sorry I couldn't come earlier," she said. "Is this a convenient time?"

"It is at that." He cleared a space on the counter. "You can bring it straight here."

Less than an hour later, Beryl was back inside the carriage and on her way to Rivenhall Park.

She tightened the drawstring opening of her overstuffed reticule as the carriage rattled to a halt in front of the main residence. She disembarked without assistance, and straightening her skirts, climbed the wide front steps.

A liveried footman greeted her at the door. "Miss Burnham. Good afternoon."

"Good afternoon. Is Sir Henry in?"

"He's in his library, ma'am."

Relief pulsed through her. She'd feared she'd tarried too long in the village, and that Henry might have already set off in pursuit of his horse. Thank goodness he was still at home.

"Will you tell him I'm here?" She stepped inside the marble-tiled hall. It was clean and cool, smelling of beeswax and lemon polish.

"Yes, ma'am." The footman waited while she divested herself of her straw bonnet and gloves. "Would you care to wait in the drawing room?"

"I'd prefer the small parlor," Beryl said.

One of the Park's rarely used reception rooms, the parlor was less Henry's domain than the drawing room or the library. She hoped that meeting him there would help to put the two of them on an equal footing.

"This way, if you please." The footman escorted her to the small silk-papered room before trotting off to fetch Henry.

Beryl paced the thickly woven blue-and-gold carpet, her arms folded at her waist. Her reticule hung heavy on her wrist.

Henry didn't make her wait. He strode into the parlor not three minutes later. His frock coat was unbuttoned, as if he'd only just shrugged it on. "Beryl."

"Henry."

He gestured for her to sit. "If you've come about that horse, you may save your breath. I've already dispatched a groom to collect him."

Beryl perched on the edge of a silk-cushioned settee. "I wish you hadn't done."

He sat down in the tufted armchair across from her, his body taut with impatience. "Your sister has given me little choice in the matter."

"Surely you must realize that she won't give him up to a mere groom. She's as likely to send the poor man away with a flea in his ear."

Henry's face clouded with barely suppressed annoyance. "Do you know what I've been doing this week? I've been sorting out the six-month tenancy agreements with my steward. Applying myself to matters that directly impact the estate, and the lives of the men and women who live and work here."

"I can appreciate that you're busy."

Henry was always busy. If not poring over papers at his desk in the library, then tramping about the grounds of the estate. The fact was, there was never a good time to call on him. Indeed, in the past, it was he who preferred to do the calling.

"Exceedingly busy." He exhaled. "Dash it all, Beryl, I don't have a moment to spare for this nonsense with your sister. Can you not make her see reason?"

"You think her unreasonable? Or merely emotional?"

"Both. She's behaving in a completely nonsensical fashion."

"Perhaps she is." Beryl folded her hands in her lap. "Love can often make people behave irrationally."

"Love for a horse?" he scoffed.

"For anyone. A family member. A friend. A much beloved pet."

"Is this supposed to inspire my compassion? Your sister is behaving like a spoiled brat."

She flinched at the insult. It wasn't like Henry to be impolite. Impatient, yes. But never rude. She supposed her sister had finally pushed him past the limits of civility. "She's behaving like a girl who loves a horse. She believes he's her perfect match."

"God save me," Henry muttered. "There's no such thing. What she believes is a girlish fancy."

"I believe it, too," Beryl said.

"You what?" Henry looked at her as if she'd spoken to him in a language he couldn't understand.

"I believe in perfect matches. In soulmates."

He shook his head. "Did you know he threw her? That she was tossed into the road in front of Malvern's Emporium?"

"It was only a minor accident. He was spooked by Mrs. Doolittle's gig. Winnifred is certain—"

"And next time? When he throws her again? When she breaks her back or her neck?"

Beryl inwardly recoiled at the prospect. One often heard of people suffering such injuries from riding. It was never pleasant to contemplate. "Isn't that a possibility with any horse?"

"Less so with a gentle mare or gelding. But with a stallion the danger increases—and Vesper's a temperamental beast. I admit she has a way with him. It's why I permitted her to exercise him. That was my mistake. He's too much horse for her."

"I don't agree."

"You would risk her health?"

"Everything's a risk, isn't it? We all might hurt ourselves doing something or other that we love. What's the alternative? To sit quietly in a parlor, attending to one's needlework? My sister is no porcelain doll, Henry. She's a vibrant, capable young woman."

"I'm not going to argue with you."

"I don't want you to argue. I want you to listen." Beryl looked into his eyes, so similar to Mark's. "You've had to exercise such control since your father died. And you've made a great success of everything here at the Park. We all of us are so very proud of you. But sometimes—sometimes, Henry, you hold onto things too tightly."

"I'm not holding onto that horse. Quite the opposite. I'm sending him back to the sales this very week."

"I don't mean the horse," she said.

Henry looked at her. Really looked at her. "My God," he said at last, "this isn't about that infernal horse, is it? This is about my brother."

She willed herself not to blush. "It's about everything. The horse and…our engagement."

His brows lowered. "What about our engagement?"

There was time enough for that. She refused to be distracted from her purpose. "Is it true that you're asking five hundred pounds for Vesper?"

"It's the amount I'm likely to get for him at the sales," Henry answered, frowning. "Beryl, what do you mean—"

"Very well." Snapping open her reticule, she withdrew a wad of folded bank notes. "I'd like to buy him."

Henry's face went ashen. "Where did you get that money?"

"It's mine," she said. "Do you accept my offer?"

"Did your aunt give you that?"

"Does it matter? It's not borrowed or stolen. It's mine absolutely, and I'm offering it to you now to purchase Vesper for my sister." She extended it to him. "Don't say you won't accept it."

"I can't accept it. Not until I know where it came from."

"Don't be absurd."

"I mean it, Beryl."

She reluctantly returned the bank notes to her reticule. "If you must know, it came from Malvern's Emporium. I sold something to Mr. Malvern just before I came here."

"For five hundred pounds?"

"You needn't sound so shocked."

"What in the world—"

"My wedding dress," she said. The reality was only now beginning to sink in. With it came a giddy feeling of freedom. "I sold my Worth wedding dress."

Chapter Twelve

*B*eryl closed the drawstring opening of her reticule, conscious of Henry's gaze fixed on her face. He appeared stunned. She didn't blame him. She still felt a little stunned herself.

When she'd visited Malvern's Emporium, she hadn't been at all confident of getting the sum she required. Granted, Aunt Hortensia had spent a small fortune on the wedding dress from Worth and Bobergh. It was a creamy white satin, stitched with tulle and swansdown, and trimmed in glass pearls and crystal beading. A dress that made Beryl look as regal as the European royalty who patronized Mr. Worth's shop.

In Paris, his designs commanded figures well over five hundred pounds. But Shepton Worthy was a long way from the continent.

"You can take it apart," Beryl had suggested to Mr. Malvern. "Learn how it was made, so that you can recreate similar styles."

"I shan't do that, Miss Burnham." Mr. Malvern had examined the wedding dress in fine detail, his attention riveted by every stitch and seam. "If this gown were mine, I'd display it in the front window. People would come for miles." He'd looked up at her, then, his eyes glittering with excitement. "Five hundred pounds, did you say?"

Beryl had felt as though she'd achieved something insurmountable. In one stroke, she'd solved both Winnifred's problem and her own.

"You sold your wedding dress," Henry said in an odd, flat voice. "Am I to take some meaning from that?"

"Yes. I wish to put an end to our betrothal."

"Because I refuse to indulge your sister?"

"Not only that." Beryl tempered her words with compassion. Henry was stuffy and frequently implacable, but he wasn't her enemy. She had no desire to be cruel. "You must see that you and I aren't suited."

He didn't reply.

She went on in spite of his silence. "It's become abundantly clear to me since returning from Paris. I could never be the wife you require. You'd only end up disappointed in me."

"Is that what's prompted this behavior? You fear I'll be disappointed in our marriage?"

"Yes, partly. But—"

"I see." He sighed heavily, looking more inconvenienced than outraged. "You're not thinking clearly. That much is plain. You've acted impulsively in selling your dress. I shall get it back for you, that goes without saying. Not but that it won't cause tongues to wag. In future, if you—"

"You can't get it back," she said. "Mr. Malvern would never sell it to you, not for any sum. He's going to display it in the window of his shop."

Henry went completely still.

Beryl's nerves jangled a warning. At last he was listening to her. At last she'd got his undivided attention. "It isn't only you I worry about disappointing. If we marry, I would be disappointed, too. I would be miserable."

"I disagree. You and I have always got on."

"Yes, we have. And I hope we'll continue to do so. But a marriage—the kind of marriage I want—must be based on more than that. There must be affection. Love."

"Such things can grow with time."

She shook her head. "I'm sorry, but they won't. Not between us. We're too—"

"It *is* Mark, isn't it?"

"I don't wish to discuss Mark."

His face hardened. He rose from his chair. "I see."

She stood as well, hands clasped in front of her. She was quite tempted to ask him what he knew of Mark's feelings for her, but she couldn't permit the discussion to take that turn, not for any amount of curiosity. She wouldn't be responsible for driving a further wedge between the two brothers. "Leave him out of it, please. This is about you and me. My decision would be the same regardless."

"Regardless of your love for him." Henry's mouth twisted in a bitter grimace. "Do you comprehend the talk this is going to cause? Will already have caused?"

"I have some notion," she said.

"Do you? Do you truly? What do you suppose the villagers are going to have to say when they see your wedding dress up on display in the front window of Malvern's Emporium? When they see you with my brother?"

"Henry, don't."

"I can weather the storm. You, on the other hand—"

"I shall weather it, too," she assured him. "In the end, it will be worth it for all of us."

"Pray it doesn't destroy you in the process." Henry walked to the marble fireplace. He stopped in front of it, standing with his back to her. His shoulders were taut beneath the lines of his frock coat. He was angry. Possibly hurt as well. She hadn't known he was capable of being hurt. "Does your mother know about this?" he asked. "Does your aunt?"

"I haven't told them yet."

"And Mark?"

Her temper flickered. "You're determined to make this about him."

"Is he aware that you're here?" Henry asked again. "That you're calling things off between us?"

"Of course not. He doesn't even know—"

"You came here first, did you? Dutiful to the last." Henry turned to face her. A muscle ticked in his cheek. "'It will pass,'" he said. "That's what I told him."

She looked up at him in confusion.

"He was young. Not long out of university. I told him that there would be time enough for courtship and marriage after he was established. I didn't comprehend the depth of the affection he held for you. That he would continue to hold for you, despite time and distance. Had I understood…" He ran a hand over his hair. "Well, it makes little difference now, does it."

Her heart thumped heavily. "For heaven's sake, Henry. If you knew how he felt, why did you propose to me?"

"Because it was the rational thing to do. You suited Rivenhall Park. You suited me. Whereas Mark's feelings…"

"You thought them irrational."

Henry shrugged. "The man who is a slave to his emotions is no man at all. I had no wish for either of my brothers to end up like our father."

Beryl felt an unwilling surge of pity for him. As the heir, he'd been shouldered with a world of burdens after his father's death. It had been his responsibility to revive the estate, and to see to the welfare of two brothers not much younger than he was himself. Henry had done that, and more. But something had been lost in the bargain. "Loving someone isn't a weakness," she said. "Even if it's wild and dangerous and defies all common sense."

His lips compressed. "And here we are again. Back at the same old argument over your sister and that horse."

"Winnifred loves him," Beryl said. "And I love her." She once again withdrew the banknotes from her reticule. "It needn't be anything more than a business transaction. Just like one you would make with a gentleman at the sales in London."

"That simple, is it?"

"If you'll let it be." When he made no move to take the money, she set it down on the small gilt desk in the corner of the parlor. "I shall leave it here. And when you are more yourself, you can draw up a bill of sale."

"More myself," Henry repeated. "You are mistaken, Miss Burnham. I am now as I ever was. As for that horse, I wish to God I'd never set eyes on him." He retrieved the banknotes, thrusting them into the inner pocket of his coat. "Forgive me, but I've spent enough time on this nonsense. My steward awaits me."

With that, he bowed and abruptly took his leave.

Beryl was left standing in the small parlor, her heart filled with a mingled sense of sorrow and relief. There was something else there, too. A longing to see Mark, so keen she fairly vibrated with the sensation.

And she would see him. Soon, but not yet.

She still had her mother and Aunt Hortensia to deal with.

"Your Worth wedding dress," Mama said. "I still can't believe it. To think it's to be displayed in the window of Malvern's Emporium like so much dirty linen."

"It's hardly that." Beryl linked her arm through her mother's as they strolled through the rose garden. It was only the two of them. Aunt Hortensia had retired to bed early, still grumbling about Beryl's duplicity, and Winnifred had returned to the stables, thrilled beyond measure at the prospect that Vesper might soon officially be hers.

"It may as well be our dirty linen we're airing," Mama said. "Everyone in the county will know why that dress is there. They'll all stop and whisper over it. You'll never be able to hold your head up again."

"People *will* talk," Beryl conceded. Ernest walked along with her, stopping intermittently to sniff at the shrubbery. It was a balmy evening, the setting sun casting a golden glow over the fragrant blooms.

She'd hoped there might be time to call at the vicarage, but the day had slipped away from her, taken up with arguments, confrontations, and an outpouring of tears. Even Winnifred had wept, though hers had been tears of joy.

"If the gossip becomes too much to bear," Mama said, "I shall persuade your aunt to take you away again."

Beryl recalled Aunt Hortensia's reaction to the news of her broken betrothal. "She isn't likely to. I'm no longer in her good graces. Far from it."

"Nonsense. You mustn't heed the things she said this evening. You gave her a shock, that's all. A woman her age doesn't like to have her plans thwarted." She squeezed Beryl's arm. "I'll speak to her in the morning. She'll soon come round."

"What about you, Mama?"

"What do you mean?"

"Are you terribly disappointed that I've called things off with Henry?"

"I am," Mama said frankly. "But not for the reasons you imagine. The loss of him won't reduce us to penury. My own income is sufficient to our needs at present, so long as we continue to live simply. As for the rest of it, your aunt occasionally provides when the whim takes her."

"Why, then?"

"Because, my dear, all I've ever wanted was for you and your sister to be favorably settled. To be safe and secure, with husbands who will take care of you after I die."

"Mama—" Beryl protested.

"No, no. It's a fact of life. I won't be here forever. And when I'm gone, you and Winnie will be left to shift for yourselves, with precious little of my money remaining to see you through the years ahead. You'll need a man's protection. Sir Henry is stern and humorless, I realize, but he seemed as wise a choice for you as any. I believe you thought so too at one time."

"I did." It was a decision Beryl had made with her head instead of her heart. One born of pragmatism, not love. "I know myself a little better now."

"Will you be happier without him?" Mama asked.

"I believe I shall. But it wasn't only marrying Henry that made me unhappy. I've always had moments of sadness. You know that. I expect I always will."

"Your father was just the same."

Beryl looked at her mother with a start. "Was he? I don't remember that."

"Oh yes. There were times he was quite low. He would take to his bookroom for hours on end. It was all I could do to induce a laugh from him." Her mouth curved in a regretful smile. "It isn't what I wanted for you. You were meant for better things. A better life than I've given you."

"Oh, Mama."

"You and your sister both. My two beautiful girls." She sighed. "If only the pair of you weren't plagued by such turmoil. I never know what might happen from one moment to the next."

Winnifred chose that moment to make her disheveled appearance. Her riding habit was covered in horse hair. Broken bits of straw clung to her silver-blond tresses. "Beryl!" She came toward them from the direction of the stables, a small parcel clutched in her hands. "A footman just brought this from Rivenhall Park."

Slipping her arm free of her mother's, Beryl went to meet her sister. "What is it?"

"I don't know. I haven't opened it yet." Winnifred extended it to her. "It's meant for you."

Mama joined them, her brow creased with apprehension. "Pray it isn't a legal document of some sort. Your aunt claims that Sir Henry would be within his rights to sue for breach of promise."

"He wouldn't dare," Winnifred said. "Imagine the scandal."

"Winnie's right. Henry would never do such a thing." Beryl tore open the parcel. Inside were several sheets of paper wrapped around a thick stack of bank notes. Her brows knit with confusion. "It's the money I gave him."

Winnifred pressed closer. "What does the letter say? He hasn't refused to sell Vesper, has he?"

Beryl's gaze moved swiftly over Henry's familiar script. "He says that he's enclosed my five hundred pounds. That he's returning it to me, along with Vesper's papers, and that I may consider..." The words died on her lips.

Winnifred took the note from Beryl's hand. "'I am returning it to you, along with papers of ownership for the hunter stallion known as Vesper. He is yours to do with as you will. Consider him a—'" She broke off in bewilderment. "'A wedding gift'? But I thought you'd called things off?"

"I have," Beryl said.

Mama's face clouded with growing alarm. "Then who is it exactly that he thinks you're marrying?"

"As to that..." Beryl gave her mother and sister an apologetic look. "I suspect he's referencing his brother."

Chapter Thirteen

*M*ark sat on a fallen tree trunk in the small wilderness garden outside the vicarage, his head resting in his hands. Since returning from the Grange yesterday afternoon, he hadn't had a moment's peace. In addition to paperwork, and other regular parish duties, he'd had countless demands on his time. He'd had to arrange for someone to help Mrs. Priddy with her laundry business. There had been a dispute to resolve between two of the ladies on the committee for the summer fete. And then, in the early evening, Mr. Venable's health had taken a turn for the worse.

Dr. Black had been summoned immediately. "He may have a difficult night," he'd said. "I advise you to sit with him."

Mark had done that, and more. He'd sponged the old vicar's brow and fed him sips of weak tea. Venable was much recovered this morning. Bundled in front of a blazing fire, he was presently engaged in reading his favorite passages from *Fordyce's Sermons to Young Men*.

Sunlight glinted through the leaves. The whisper of a breeze, and the sound of birds singing softly settled Mark's agitated spirits.

Good lord. Had he really told Beryl that he loved her?

It had been stupid. Foolish. A worthless confession, achieving nothing save to make them both uncomfortable in each other's company.

But he couldn't permit himself to dwell on it. Couldn't let himself sink into a despondency. Beryl had had the right of it. Such emotions were better left unspoken.

Now, if only he could stop feeling them. Could stop himself from thinking of her.

She was so much on his mind that, when he looked up and saw her coming toward him through the woods, he thought he must be dreaming.

Ernest soon shattered that possibility with a flurry of shrill barks. He trotted ahead of Beryl on the path, his plumed tail held high, like the black flag of a marauding pirate ship.

"Beryl." Mark leapt to his feet, conscious of his state of undress. He was absent his frock coat, his shirtsleeves rolled up and his waistcoat only partially buttoned. His hair stood half on end. He ran a hand over it in a futile attempt to put himself in order. "What are you doing here?"

She was wearing one of her light-colored muslin day dresses. An old gown. It was soft and faded, giving her the look of a simple village girl.

A *beautiful* village girl.

"I hope I'm not intruding?"

"No. Not at all. I was just..." He trailed off as she came to a halt in front of him.

"I called at the vicarage. Mrs. Phillips said you'd gone for a walk. I thought you might be here."

"Is everything all right?" He'd left her in the midst of a family drama with her sister and Henry. Lord only knew how things had been resolved. With a great many tears, probably. Winnifred wouldn't have let the horse go easily.

"Perfectly fine." She glanced at the fallen tree. "May I sit with you here?"

"By all means." He waited while she sat down before taking a seat next to her. "Did everything get sorted out with the horse?"

"Indeed," she said. "To everyone's satisfaction."

His brows lifted. "Even Winnifred's?"

She smiled. "Henry made her a gift of Vesper. She's over the moon, as you can imagine."

Mark had to tighten his jaw to prevent it falling open. "*Gave* him to her? And this is my brother we're talking about?"

"Yes, I know. It was exceedingly generous of him."

Generous wasn't the word that came to mind. Unhinged was more like it. Uncharacteristic to the point of abnormal. "How ever did you convince him to change his mind?"

"Ah. As to that…it's rather complicated." Her smile faded slowly. "I'd have told you all about it yesterday, but there was no way I could get away from home. Mama and Aunt Hortensia weren't in the best of moods."

"Understandably so, given your sister's behavior."

"Oh no. They'd quite forgotten Winnifred's capers by the evening. It was me they were upset with."

Mark frowned. He searched her face. "You? What for?"

"I'm afraid I let them down quite badly. I surprised them as well, which Aunt Hortensia informs me is even worse at her age. They were rather glum last night, but I have every hope that they'll rally. Indeed, they're not unreasonable people. And they do love me, and want me to be happy."

His senses sharpened. "Beryl, what did you—"

"I'm not going to marry Henry."

"*What?*" He stared at her.

"I broke things off with him. And it hasn't anything to do with you. Well…not entirely." She paused. "After we kissed, it *was* difficult to imagine marrying Henry. I hadn't known how different kisses could be until then."

His gaze was riveted to hers. Good lord. *Good lord.* "You're not going to marry him."

"No." Her mouth tilted slightly at one corner. "How could I when I love someone else?"

Everything within Mark stilled, his emotions poised on a knife's edge of hope and despair. He didn't dare speak. Didn't dare breathe. His entire world stopped spinning on its axis, reduced to a single point. To *her*.

Her expression softened with rueful tenderness. "I love you, Mark. I've always loved you. But I didn't realize until I came home from Paris that it was something even more than that."

He swallowed hard. "What could be more?"

"I fell in love with you." She reached to cup his cheek, cradling his face in the palm of her slim hand. "I'm *in* love with you."

His voice went hoarse with emotion. "You never let on."

"I didn't know it myself. It happened so gradually. Somewhere between that first letter you wrote to me and the day I came to your office. The day you gave me that journal. I was never so aware of you as I was then. And then…when you kissed me." The pad of her thumb brushed over his cheekbone in a fleeting caress. "But you must have felt it, too."

"I did. All of it. All of those feelings." He covered her hand with his. "I'm in love with you something fierce."

A spasm of emotion crossed over her face. Her body listed toward him. A subtle movement, hardly discernable, but one he couldn't ignore. Drawing her hand from his cheek, he pressed a kiss to her palm, and another to her wrist. And then he gathered her in his arms.

Her own arms wound tight around his neck, her skirts billowing over his legs in a sea of faded cotton and crinoline. She clung to him. And when his lips found hers, she kissed him back. Softly, deeply. Kissed him and kissed him, with a yielding sweetness that swiftly robbed him of his senses.

He buried his face in the curve of her neck. She smelled of sunshine and elderflowers. Of summer days under a clear blue sky. "How I've wanted this."

"What have you wanted?" Her breath was a teasing whisper against his ear.

"This." He kissed her again, feeling her fingers tangle in his hair. "And this." His lips brushed the satiny slope of her cheek, and the smooth curve of her brow. "I've wanted you. Longed for you. A day hasn't passed that I haven't dreamed of taking you in my arms. Of kissing you here. And here."

"*Mark.*"

The breathless sound of his name on her lips was nearly his undoing. His cheek came to rest against hers. "I'm desperate for you," he confessed. "Afraid that any moment Venable is going to come and wake me."

"You think this is another dream?"

He huffed a laugh. "If it is, it's better than any I've ever had."

She slowly drew back, her hands sliding from his shoulders to rest on his chest. "I'm not a dream. I'm all too human."

Mark gazed down at her. He wanted to kiss her again. To hold her. To stay with her here forever. A lifetime wouldn't be long enough. "You, my dear Miss Burnham, are my golden girl."

"I mean it, Mark. I'm not perfect. If you put me on a pedestal, you'll only be disappointed. You above all people should know that."

He smoothed her hair. "What's this about?"

"I don't want you to have false expectations. You've seen me at my worst. You know how bad it can be."

"I love *you*, Beryl." It was so much an understatement it felt like a lie. Love was too simple a word for what he felt for her. He could never fully express it, this emotion so powerful and precious. It was as elemental as fire. As enduring as the stones that formed the bed of the Worthy. "I love you for everything that you are. The dark and the light."

Her eyes glistened. "Sometimes, I fear that the darkness may eclipse the light entirely."

"Well, then." He smiled. "It's lucky you'll have me at your side, an oil lamp at the ready."

Her mouth trembled on a reluctant smile. "It will have to be a very powerful one."

"Light is always more powerful than darkness."

"That's the clergyman in you talking."

Mark couldn't deny it. His faith was as much a part of him as his love for her. "I can't make the melancholy go away. You know that as well as I. But I promise to be there for you when it comes. To hold you in my arms. To read Dickens to you and make you laugh." His hand moved over the curve of her spine. "I'll be with you. You'll never again have to face this demon alone."

She settled back against him, reassured by his touch. "I wish you could be with me always."

"I can." He rested his chin atop her head. "If we—"

"Don't speak of it," she said softly. "Not yet."

Mark's muscles tensed. "Why not? I thought—"

"I know. It's what I want, too. But I've been free of Henry for less than a day. If you and I act too quickly, it will cause even more of a scandal in the village. We must tread carefully. Otherwise…I fear we'll hurt him. And worse."

He pulled back just enough to look her in the eye. "What could be worse?"

"We'll damage your position as curate at the very moment you're about to be elevated to vicar."

Mark's spirits plummeted. A purely selfish part of him wanted to laugh. To say that he didn't care about his position in the church. That he would marry her tomorrow if she would have him. To the devil with scandal—and with Henry. Mark had waited for her long enough.

But she was right, of course.

He couldn't very well pay court to her the day after she'd jilted his brother. It would be callous. Thoughtless and cruel—both to Henry and to her. Had he been thinking clearly, he would have realized that for himself.

His chest tightened with misery as he reluctantly set her away from him. "How long?"

She looked as unhappy as he felt. "I don't know. How long do you think would be appropriate?"

"Six months?" He could barely bring himself to suggest it. It would mean waiting all the way through Christmas and into the New Year.

It felt like an eternity.

"Six months." She slid her hands into his. "Surely that won't be too terrible? Not if we love each other."

"I do love you." He brought her hands to his lips. "And I shall wait for you forever if I have to. But," he added, "that doesn't mean I have to like it."

Chapter Fourteen

*M*ark crossed the busy village green. The day of the Shepton Worthy summer fete had dawned bright with promise. Indeed, he was feeling extraordinarily optimistic. The sun was shining, the sky was clear, and a rail journey to Taunton the previous day had proved particularly fruitful. He carried the evidence of that fact tucked safely away in the inner pocket of his coat. All that was left was to speak to Beryl.

He passed between two rows of stalls decorated with flowers and greenery. They were doing a steady business selling cakes and preserves, knitted goods, and needlework. Colorful banners were strung overhead, fluttering in the breeze, and in the distance musicians performed on a raised wooden platform. The notes of a raucous jig sounded through the air, punctuated by shouts and laughter.

Beryl's stall was ahead. She was leaning out of it, speaking to one of the villagers as they examined her whitework. Her golden hair glinted in the sun.

Mark's pulse quickened. He'd seen her only once since returning from Taunton. She'd been at the church yesterday afternoon, along with the other members of the ladies' committee, finalizing plans for the fete.

There had been no chance to be private with her. No opportunity to kiss her or to hold her in his arms. To tell her again that he loved her. He'd begun to long for such intimate moments, brief though they must be.

"Rivenhall!" Simon Black emerged from the crowd. He was hatless, wearing a light sack coat with a pair of plaid trousers. His fair hair was combed into meticulous order. "How was Taunton?"

"Surprisingly agreeable," Mark replied, stopping to greet him.

"Parish business, was it?"

Mark's mouth tilted up at one corner. "Something like that."

"I'm glad you're back, at any rate. There's been some gossip brewing about Miss Burnham's betrothal to Sir Henry having been broken."

"Has there." It was inevitable, Mark supposed. There were no secrets in a small village, and if there were, people didn't keep them long.

"Is it true?" Black asked.

"It is," Mark admitted. "But there's been no announcement to that effect."

"You haven't seen it then."

"Seen what?"

"The wedding dress in the window at Malvern's Emporium."

Mark started. Good lord. Had Malvern displayed it already? Beryl had told Mark about the draper's intentions, but Mark hadn't expected the man to act so quickly. "When did he put it up?"

"Just this morning. I saw it when I was leaving my offices, bold as you please. I expect he's trying to capitalize on the crowds generated by the fete."

Mark's gaze found Beryl again. She was too far away to tell for certain, but it seemed she was in good spirits. Perhaps no one had yet had the temerity to mention it to her?

"That isn't the only reason I was hoping we might cross paths," Black said.

"Oh?" Mark asked, distracted. "I trust nothing is amiss with one of your patients?"

"You might say that." Black's countenance turned serious. "I've had word that Bert Priddy has been seen in the village."

Mark gave him an alert look. "When?"

"This morning. He was spotted staggering about down by the smithy. I feared he'd gone home to cause more mischief, but when I stopped by the Priddys' cottage, it was empty. Mrs. Priddy was either gone or—"

"Mrs. Priddy is here," Mark said. "I saw her earlier, assisting one of the ladies at their cake stall."

"And what about her husband? You don't think he'd show his face at the fete?"

Mark frowned. "He may well. Old Mr. Hinchcliffe is selling his cider. It has a reputation for being stronger than advertised." Indeed, his stall was already drawing crowds, just as it did every year. Mark cast a glance over the queue. "I don't see him yet. I'll keep a lookout."

"As will I." Black fell in at Mark's side as he resumed walking. "Have you spoken to Sir Henry about it yet?"

Guilt pricked at Mark's conscience. "I haven't had the opportunity."

He'd meant to do it on Wednesday, but Beryl had arrived at the vicarage. Had told him that she loved him. That she was *in* love with him. The rest of the world had faded away. Since then, he'd been wary of facing Henry. But it would have to be done, for Mrs. Priddy's sake if not for his own— and sooner rather than later.

"I'll call on him at the Park this evening," Mark said. "We'll have more privacy there."

Black nodded. "Let me know what he says."

"Are you staying to enjoy the fete?"

"Until I'm summoned to attend to some injury or other incurred in the course of the day."

"In my experience," Mark said, "the fete doesn't produce any sick or injured until closer to sunset, and that's usually owing to Mr. Hinchcliffe's cider. You're safe enough for now."

"In that case"—Black quirked a wry smile—"I'll make a brief foray into the tea tent."

It billowed ahead of them at the top of the green, the flap pinned open to reveal a smattering of small wooden card tables and chairs. A few ladies and gentleman were seated inside, drinking tea and eating sugared buns.

"I believe Miss Winnifred is one of the ladies doling out refreshments this year," Mark warned him. "If that affects your decision."

"I'm aware." Black tugged at his shirt collar—an uncharacteristically self-conscious gesture. "Once more unto the breach," he muttered before striding off.

Watching him duck into the tea tent, it was all Mark could do to contain a laugh. So, it was like that, was it? He felt a fool for not having realized it before.

He wondered what else he'd missed among the members of his parish. He'd been so besotted with Beryl—so twisted in knots over her marriage to Henry—that he'd been incapable of seeing straight.

But things were different now.

Everything was different.

He made his way toward Beryl's stall. Her arms were folded on the ledge of it, the bell-shaped sleeves of her summer day dress pillowing there in a froth of fabric.

As he drew closer, she cast a look in his direction. Catching sight of him at last, her mouth curved in a smile. It illuminated her entire face, sparking an answering glow within Mark's breast.

He smiled back at her. A foolish, besotted smile, no doubt. He lengthened his stride, but before he could reach her, a villager moving in the opposite direction shoved past him, slamming hard against his shoulder. An aroma of sour sweat and gin followed after the man.

Mark turned to confront him and came face-to-face with Bert Priddy.

His clothing was rumpled, his filthy hair partially covered by a ragged woolen cap. He wasn't a small man. He was a big bruiser of a fellow, not much older than forty if Mark was to guess.

"Mr. Priddy," he said. "Where are you off to in such a hurry?"

Priddy gave him a sullen glare. "Looking for my wife, ain't I."

"That's the cider stall you're headed for," Mark pointed out.

"No crime in having a drink first."

It looked as though he'd already had several. He wasn't a very nice man when he was drunk. Quite the opposite. There was no telling what havoc he might wreak.

"You and I need to talk," Mark said grimly. "Shall we go into the church?"

"Ain't going to no church. And won't countenance your meddling, Curate. This is between me and my missus."

"There you're wrong. When you harm someone weaker than yourself—"

"She's my wife."

"And should therefore be treated with respect." Mark's voice roughened with suppressed anger. "You broke her arm. Battered her face. Left her with no means to make her living."

Priddy waved the accusations away as he moved to walk past. "I never did nothing to that woman."

Mark blocked his path. "Shall I summon the doctor to recount her injuries?"

"Ah, what a load of—"

"You deny that you struck her?"

"It's none of your business."

"It is when you're a tenant of Rivenhall Park." Mark shouldn't have said it. He had nothing to do with Henry's tenancy agreements. No say in estate matters at all. Had Priddy not been so provoking, Mark might have kept his mouth shut. As it was, he knew at once that he'd gone too far. A threat to a man's tenancy was a threat to his home, his very hope of survival.

Priddy's large fists clenched at his sides. "I pay my rents." His words grew loud with belligerence. "You ask that man of Sir Henry's. He'll tell you."

Some of the villagers stopped to stare. There were whispers and even a giggle or two.

"There's no need to make a scene," Mark said. "We can talk at the church."

"I won't be preached at," Priddy said. "Don't care who your brother is."

"Come." Mark took Priddy's elbow to encourage him away from the fete. "It will give you time to sober up."

Priddy jerked free of Mark's grasp, and without warning, punched him in the face.

Mark's head snapped back. Stars exploded behind his eyes. He staggered back a step, but quickly regained his footing, more surprised than hurt.

"Out of my way," Priddy said. "Unless you want more of the same."

Mark was vaguely conscious of blood trickling from his nose. He ignored it. Mrs. Priddy had endured far worse. "I'm not going anywhere." He continued to bar the man's path, preventing him from storming off to find his wife. "Indeed, I think it's time you learned what happens when you pick a fight with someone your own size."

"I said out of the way." Priddy swung again.

This time, Mark was ready. He sidestepped Priddy's fist, and drawing back his own, struck a blow squarely across Priddy's jaw. It landed with an ominous thud.

Priddy dropped like a felled oak, grunting as he hit the ground.

Astonished gasps echoed through the crowd of onlookers. Some of the men cheered. "That's it, Curate! You show him!"

Another fellow exclaimed, "A leveler if ever I saw one!"

Priddy's face bore the expression of a stunned animal. He'd plainly never faced any consequences for his violence—physical or otherwise. He struggled back to his feet. "Why, you—"

Mark didn't wait for him to rally. He used the opportunity to take hold of Priddy's outstretched arm and twist it behind his back. "That's enough," he said quietly. "We'll be going now."

Priddy fought and shouted, cursing Mark for all to hear as Mark marched him away from the fete. Mark had gotten no farther than the other side of the green when a familiar voice stopped him short.

"It seems you need a little help."

Mark's head jerked up to find his brother beside him. "I have things under control."

"What's he done?" Henry asked.

"He's drunk—violently drunk. When he was last in this condition, he nearly killed his wife."

Henry's lips flattened. "I think a trip to the cells might be in order."

Priddy objected strenuously. "I ain't done nothing," he cried, attempting to shake free of Mark's grasp.

"I don't look favorably on men who beat their wives," Henry informed him.

"Nor I," Mark said, tightening his grip on Priddy's arm.

"You're a tenant of mine, aren't you?" Henry asked. "I thought you looked familiar."

At that, Priddy hung his head. Some of the fight went out of him. He weakly asserted his innocence once more before falling silent.

Henry summoned two nearby villagers. "Take him to the gaol. Tell the constable I'll be there directly."

Mark relinquished Priddy into the custody of the two brawny men. Perhaps it was for the best. There would be no talking to him in his current condition.

Henry remained with Mark as the men led Priddy away. "That was a rather robust display of Christianity," he said. "I don't recall Venable ever ministering to his flock in such a fashion."

Mark might have smiled if his face didn't hurt so much. "I don't intend to make a habit of it." He withdrew his handkerchief to wipe the blood from his nose.

Henry watched with a strangely solemn expression. "Have a care in future, will you? You're the only brother I've got."

Mark was surprised by the ring of sincerity in his brother's words. "After recent events, I'd have thought you'd be glad to be rid of me."

"Give me some credit. I know enough to admit when I've been wrong."

Mark dropped his hand from his face, his bloody handkerchief still clenched in his fingers. It occurred to him that Priddy's punch might have rattled his brain loose. Surely Henry hadn't just said what Mark had thought he did. "Wrong about what?"

"About you. About her."

The admission sank into Mark's soul. "I love her," he said. "I've loved her for years, unrelenting. I know you thought it was something fleeting and foolish, but—"

"I was the one who was foolish." Henry's mouth twisted into a grimace. "I won't say I'm completely at peace with the way things have transpired. But it isn't because I don't care for you. Despite what you might think, I do want you to be happy."

Mark was deeply moved by Henry's words. He hadn't expected them. Hadn't realized how much he needed to hear them. "Thank you. That means a great deal."

Henry's gaze was caught by something beyond Mark's shoulder. "Speaking of your happiness…"

Mark turned his head. Beryl was walking briskly toward him, Ernest trotting along at the hem of her skirts. Her face was a picture of concern.

"She never looked at me like that," Henry observed. He didn't sound hurt by the fact, merely reflective.

Mark nevertheless felt a flicker of sympathy for him. "I wish I could say I was sorry, but—"

"Quite so. She's yours now. I believe she's always been yours." Henry clapped Mark on the shoulder before taking his leave. "You'll understand if I don't linger."

Chapter Fifteen

"Are you all right?" Beryl lifted her hand to Mark's face, her touch infinitely gentle.

Mark gazed down at her, a hint of a smile on his lips. "I'm fine," he said. "It's nothing."

Beryl didn't know about that. She hadn't seen the fight from her stall. The crowd around Mark and Mr. Priddy had been too heavy. But it hadn't taken but a few moments for someone to gleefully relate the details to her. "If it's nothing, why was Henry with you?"

"He was assisting with Bert Priddy. They've taken him to the gaol."

Music and laughter floated on the air behind them. Gigs and open carts were still arriving at the green, villagers and their young families spilling out, anxious to take part in the eating, drinking, and children's theatricals on offer at the fete.

Beryl wasn't feeling very festive at present. "Mrs. Doolittle claims that you knocked him down."

"A minor altercation. Priddy was drunk." Mark paused, adding, "And he struck the first blow."

"Your nose is bleeding," she said.

"Ah. Sorry about that." He dabbed at it with his handkerchief. "I should go back to the vicarage and clean up."

"I'll go with you." Beryl picked up Ernest. It wasn't far to the church. They crossed from the green to the street, walking the short distance to the churchyard. "I wonder what Mr. Venable will say?"

"Pray he won't notice." Mark opened the gate. Climbing roses caught at Beryl's muslin skirts as she passed through. He followed after her, shutting the gate behind him. "Venable doesn't approve of brawling."

Beryl huffed. The very idea of Mark engaging in a brawl. It beggared belief. Not because he was weak. Indeed, with his commanding height and leanly muscled frame, he was more than capable of handling all comers. Despite that, she'd never once witnessed him commit an act of violence. Never seen him be anything but kind and compassionate.

But there was strength, even in that. A power in his compassion, stronger than mere physicality. It made her love him all the more.

She dropped Ernest onto the grass. "Isn't there a pump here somewhere?"

"Behind the church."

"That will suffice." She crossed the empty churchyard with Mark at her heels. At the back of the church, a weathered wooden bench stood near a cluster of crumbling gravestones. "Sit down," she said. "I'll be right back."

She didn't wait for him to comply. Finding the pump, she used it to soak her white linen handkerchief. When she returned, Mark was seated on the bench, waiting. He'd removed his coat. It was draped next to him.

She sat down at his side, her skirts pooling around his legs. "Let me see." Turning his face toward hers with a soft brush of her fingers, she wiped away the last remnants of blood.

His gaze rested on her face as she worked. "You'll ruin your handkerchief."

She gave him a look. As if she cared one jot for her linens when the man she loved was injured. "You don't think he broke your nose, do you?"

"No. It's fine. Truly."

She blotted his lip and the edge of his cheek. "The bleeding seems to have stopped, at least. You'll be fit enough to face Mr. Venable."

Mark didn't appear unduly worried. "Is that another damselfly?"

She lowered her handkerchief to examine the small white-work figure in the corner. When wet, the thread was almost invisible. "It is."

He smiled. "Hiding in plain sight."

"Not hiding. You noticed it."

His fingers gently encircled her wrist, the pad of his thumb resting on her pulse. It leapt at his touch. "Beryl—"

"My wedding dress is in the window of the Emporium," she blurted out.

"I know." Mark's smile faded. It was replaced by a look of concern. "Are you—"

"I'm perfectly well," she said.

It wasn't entirely true.

The whispers about her broken betrothal had already begun to catch flame. Beryl had sensed the gossip swirling in the air as she stood inside her stall at the fete, selling her whitework. Several village ladies had stopped, not to buy but to talk, their chitchat sprinkled with wheedling innuendo.

She wondered what people would say when they learned that it wasn't only a broken betrothal? That it was Mark she loved, not Henry?

It was going to be a trial by fire. She would have to be brave. And she could be if she needed to. That much, she'd proven to herself already. She'd sold her dress and confronted Henry. Had even managed to procure Winnifred a horse. And she'd done it alone.

What more might she accomplish with Mark at her side?

"Are you certain?" he asked.

"I'm not afraid of the gossip," she said. "What does it signify what any of them say? They none of them have a connection to my own happiness. Yours is the only opinion that matters to me." She hesitated. "You're not put off by it, are you?"

"No. All I care about is you." His thumb moved over her wrist. "I wanted to see you alone today. To talk with you about something."

Warmth suffused her veins as he caressed her hand. "What about?"

"I'm not sure now is the right time. Everything was meant to be perfect."

She returned the clasp of his fingers. Her mouth curved. "This isn't perfect?"

He bent his head to hers. "In a graveyard, with you ministering to my wounds?" Humor sounded in his voice, along with masculine chagrin. "It's not the way I envisioned it."

Nearby, a soft snore rose from Ernest as he dozed peacefully in the sun. He'd worn himself out at the fete, barking at every villager who passed.

"I think it's lovely here," she said. "It's a beautiful day. The wildflowers are blooming. And we're here, alone together, outside the church. Not far from the place you first kissed me."

Mark looked at her steadily.

"Tell me," she urged him.

"Very well. If you insist." After a long moment, he drew back. "You said you didn't want me to mention marriage. Because of Henry. That it was better for us to wait for a certain length of time."

"Six months, we agreed." It felt like forever. And even then, Beryl doubted the gossip would have died down.

"Exactly. But that doesn't mean we can't talk about the future, does it? Just you and I, privately together. It would hurt no one if we began to make plans."

Her brows knit. "No…I suppose not."

He seemed relieved at her answer. "Good. Because I wanted to tell you that there's a fair chance I might leave Shepton Worthy."

The color drained from her face. "You're leaving?"

"I didn't mean you." He took her hands in both of his, holding them safe. "I would never leave you. I meant my position here as curate."

Relief washed over her. Still, she didn't understand. Mark had been born in Shepton Worthy. Had lived here all of his life. It was his home. "But why?"

"It would be for the best. For both of us. Think of it—a new parish. A place where we could start over with a clean slate. And it wouldn't be too far from your mother and sister, nor even from Henry."

"You sound as though you have another church in mind."

"I do. The living at the Earl of Harbury's estate in Dorset stands vacant. Dr. Black has written to him on my behalf, and if matters progress as he believes they will—"

"What has Dr. Black to do with it?"

Mark hesitated before answering. "Lord Harbury is his father. It's something Black prefers to keep private."

Beryl blinked. "My goodness." Winnifred had claimed Dr. Black was opposed to the aristocracy. Yet, here he was, the son of an actual earl. "And he's confident his father will offer the living to you?"

"He is."

A vicarage in Dorset. Beryl could already picture it in her mind. A place where she and Mark could be together, free from the unhappy associations of the past. The prospect thrilled her. Was it truly possible? To leave Shepton Worthy and its gossip behind? It would mean leaving Mama and Winnifred, too. But Mark was right. Dorset wasn't far. There would be no difficulty in seeing her family.

Could this truly be what he wanted?

"What about Mr. Venable?" she asked. "His health is getting no better. He surely won't last longer than a twelve-month. You've been waiting so long to become vicar here." She could only think of one reason Mark would have changed his mind. The very notion of it made her bristle. "Is this because of Henry? Has he said you can't have the living?"

"Not explicitly, no. He did reference it once. I was angry with him, but since then, I've been giving it a great deal of thought. Settling so close to Rivenhall Park, being dependent on my brother for my livelihood…it isn't ideal. And it's going to become less so when I marry."

"Because of me."

Mark didn't deny it.

Her stomach twisted into a knot. "I won't come between the two of you. Not any more than I already have."

"Beryl—"

"If you married someone else—"

His grip on her hands tightened. "There is no one else. There is *never* going to be anyone else. Not if I live to be one hundred and five. Don't you see? Henry doesn't matter. Shepton Worthy doesn't matter. All that matters is that we're together. I would rather live with you at the edge of the world than be without you for another second."

"You feel that way now, but—" Her insecurities briefly bubbled to the surface. "What if I can't be a good wife to you? What if there are days when my melancholy is too much for you to bear? A vicar's wife should be without fault. And I'm not. I'm flawed. Deeply flawed. In time, you might regret having married me."

An expression of profound tenderness stole over his face. He squeezed her hands before letting them go. "I think we're putting the cart before the horse."

The loss of his touch left her oddly bereft. She folded her hands in her lap, her cheeks heating with burgeoning mortification. Here she was talking about her inadequacies as his wife, and he hadn't even proposed to her. "You're right," she said. "I'm being precipitate."

"We both are. Which brings me to the real reason I was hoping for a private moment with you today. I wanted to tell you"—Mark reached for his frock coat—"that when I was in Taunton, I learned something about mineralogy."

Mineralogy?

Beryl feigned a polite interest. "Oh?"

"There was a gentleman there in the high street who knew everything about stones." Mark withdrew something from the pocket of his frock coat. It was a small hinged box bound in pebbled leather.

Her interest was no longer feigned. "Was this gentleman, by chance, a jeweler?"

"He was." Mark presented the box to her on the palm of his hand.

She took it with trembling fingers. "Am I to open it?"

"Please."

Unhooking the brass clasp, she slowly raised the creaking lid. Inside, a ring sat on a bed of velvet. An engagement ring, she thought. But it wasn't a diamond or a garnet on the band of polished gold. It was a faceted stone of a vibrant blue-green.

"It's a beryl," Mark said. "Like you."

She touched the stone with her fingertips. "It's beautiful."

"It is, isn't it?" He admired it right along with her. "The gentleman at the jewelry shop was a veritable encyclopedia on the subject of beryls. He had every color you can imagine. Could recite chapter and verse on which was the most valuable and why." He paused. "Were you aware that a flawless beryl is completely clear? Like glass?"

Her heart beat hard. "No. I didn't know that."

"Nor did I," Mark said. "Apparently, it's the imperfections—the impurities—that give a beryl its color."

Her gaze met his.

"All the beauty you see before you is on account of the flaws. Were it perfect, it would have no color at all. No value, certainly not to me." He took the ring from its box. "I prefer this one. It matches your eyes."

His handsome face blurred in front of her. She blinked to clear her vision. She didn't want to cry. Not now. Not even from an excess of joy. She didn't want to miss a single blessed moment.

Moving from the bench, Mark sank to one knee in front of her and took her left hand gently in his. "Miss Burnham," he said with husky gravity. "I've loved you since we read Dickens together the summer you turned eighteen. I've loved you near, and far. When I thought you might be mine, and when I feared you were lost to me forever. And now—if you'll let me—I mean to love you for the remainder of my life. And beyond that, too, I suspect, if you'll consent to be my wife."

Her throat tightened with emotion.

"I know we agreed to wait six months," he said. "And we will. We needn't announce anything yet. And it would probably be best if you hid the ring away until January. But I need to know, when the time comes…will you marry me?"

The threat of tears rendered her voice the veriest raspy whisper. "Yes," she managed. "Yes, yes."

Mark's own eyes shimmered. His mouth hitched into a smile that swiftly spread into a grin. He slid the beryl ring onto her finger. No sooner had he done so than he was back at her side, and she was in his arms.

She didn't wait for him to kiss her. Curving her hand around the back of his neck, she tugged his face to hers with gentle insistence. He bent his head, and she stretched to reach him, her mouth finding his. Their breath mingled, their half-parted lips meeting and clinging.

One kiss led to another and another. They were interspersed with murmured love words and giddy huffs of laughter.

"I don't know why I'm laughing," she said. "I daresay it's because I'm so happy."

"I know you are." Mark's strong fingers brushed over the dimple in her cheek. "I'm happy, too. More than any man has a right to be."

"*Is* happiness a right?" she wondered.

"What else?"

"I think it's something we must earn. That we must fight for every day."

He smiled down at her. "And when we finally have it in our grasp?"

She moved back into his waiting arms, her own smile hidden against his chest. "We must hold on to it, of course."

Mark enfolded her in a fierce embrace. His voice was deep with certainty. "We shall."

Epilogue

Dorset, England
August 1865

Mark closed the lid of the hamper. "There's plenty more food if you're hungry."

"I couldn't eat another bite." Beryl leaned back against the curving trunk of the old oak tree, whose wide branches shielded their picnic from the midday sun. "Mrs. Fraser always packs too much."

Their housekeeper at the Harbury Court vicarage was a hearty, motherly sort of woman. She enjoyed nothing more than looking after the pair of them. Indeed, Beryl and Mark had been welcomed and accepted by all of the villagers in Harbury Norton, most of whom seemed to take a special pride in their handsome new vicar and his equally new bride.

"Sometimes," Mark said, "I suspect Mrs. Fraser enjoys our Monday picnics as much as we do."

"She's a romantic." Beryl paused, adding, "As are you."

"I won't deny it."

Their Monday picnics had been his idea. Saturdays were taken up with writing his sermons, and Sundays belonged to his parishioners. But Mondays were Beryl's exclusively.

He stretched out on the picnic blanket, his head pillowed in her lap. He'd already removed his coat and loosened his cravat. Clad in his shirtsleeves, a black cloth waistcoat, and trousers, he looked perfectly at his ease.

She smoothed his dark hair from his brow. There was something endlessly pleasurable about the liberties she was allowed to take as his wife. She could touch him whenever she wished—and with as much familiarity as she wished. He was hers, absolutely. A heady sensation, and one Mark seemed to relish as much as she did herself.

A drowsy quiet stretched between them. It was a peaceful silence, born of trust and understanding. They'd been married all of six months. Hardly any time at all. But it felt as though they'd been together for far longer.

"What are you thinking about, my love?" he asked.

A smile touched her lips. "I was thinking how lucky I am to have married my best friend."

Mark's blue gaze softened. He caught her hand in his and pressed a kiss to it.

"And what about you?" she asked.

"I was thinking about how much I'm going to miss our Monday picnics."

"The summer isn't over yet."

"No, but when the weather changes…" His mouth hitched up at one corner. "We shall have to take our picnics indoors."

Warmth crept into her cheeks. Best friends they might be, but their marriage didn't lack for passion. It was a part of their relationship she'd come to enjoy far more than she'd been led to believe she would. Their wedding night had been a revelation in that regard, just as Mark's kisses had been so many months before. She'd learned very quickly that intimacy wasn't something to be endured. On the contrary, with the right person—the right partner—it could be something extraordinary.

"Indoor picnics aren't entirely without their charms," she said.

"No, indeed. They have many things to recommend them." His fingers threaded through hers. "Privacy, for one."

"We have privacy here." The oak tree was situated on a secluded knoll, about a mile's walk from the vicarage. It wasn't wholly invisible to prying eyes, but very nearly. "And we have the sun shining so beautifully. I don't want to think of winter coming. Not yet."

"You're right, of course. We must enjoy this moment while we can."

"A moment 'of unmixed happiness,'" she said.

His eyes twinkled. "*Pickwick* again?"

"It seems suitable."

"Eminently suitable." He quoted to her from the same closing passage of Mr. Dickens's novel: "'There are dark shadows on the earth, but its lights are stronger in the contrast.'"

Beryl looked out across the Dorset hills. The day was warm and bright, the sky a startling shade of cerulean blue. A glow of contentment spread through her. Her new life wasn't perfect, but it was something very like it. There *were* moments of unmixed happiness. Of all-consuming joy. Moments like this one.

And there was Mark—her friend, her beloved, the companion of her heart.

"I believe that," she said. "I know it to be true."

Mark drew their linked hands to rest on his midsection. His clasp was strong and sure. "So do I."

Author's Note

The title of this story was inspired by William Wordsworth's 1798 poem *She Dwelt Among the Untrodden Ways*. The subject of the poem, a beautiful young maid named Lucy, lives out her life unseen, unknown, and very much alone. Beryl Burnham is living in a similar state—though her condition isn't as obvious to the casual observer. As someone who suffers from clinical depression, her loneliness is largely an internal concern. She isn't truly known or understood by anyone until she shares her burden with Mark Rivenhall.

I've briefly touched on Victorian views on melancholy in some of my earlier novels, often to Gothic effect; however, there's nothing Gothic about the melancholy that Beryl suffers from in *Fair as a Star*. She's an ordinary person, just trying to get through the day. Her experience is my effort at depicting the real impact of living with depression in an era where it wasn't entirely understood, and where the available treatments swung wildly between two extremes: relatively harmless quackery and the physical and mental abuse perpetrated in Victorian asylums.

As for Mark, his approach to Beryl's illness is very much based on common sense, and aided by his experience as a clergyman. He understands the value that Beryl can find in unburdening herself—whether to him or by writing in her journal. He also communicates with Beryl through their shared love of Charles Dickens's novels. Dickens was, without a doubt, the most popular novelist of the period, but I chose him for this story mainly for the pleasure of quoting from his 1837 novel *The Pickwick Papers* (originally published in serial form as *The Posthumous Papers of the Pickwick Club*). The passage that Mark and Beryl reference in the Epilogue is one that I find as beautiful as it is applicable:

> Let us leave our old friend in one of those moments of unmixed happiness, of which, if we seek them, there are ever some, to cheer our transitory existence here. There are dark shadows on the earth, but its lights are stronger in the contrast. Some men, like bats or owls, have better eyes for the darkness than for the light. We, who have no such optical powers, are better pleased to take our last parting look at the visionary companions of many solitary hours, when the brief sunshine of the world is blazing full upon them.

If you'd like more information on Victorian melancholy, or on any of the other subjects featured in *Fair as a Star* (Worth gowns, fancy needlework, etc.), please visit the blog portion of my author website at MimiMatthews.com.

Acknowledgments

I'm so grateful to everyone who guided and supported me during the writing of this book. Special thanks to Flora, Lena, and Alissa for reading early versions of the story, and to my editor, Deb Nemeth, whose opinion I respect and rely on so very much.

Thanks are also due to my cover designer, James Egan; to Colleen Sheehan for formatting; and—as always—to my wonderful parents.

Lastly, I'd like to thank you, my readers. Your kindness and encouragement mean the world to me. I appreciate you all more than words can say.

About the Author

USA Today bestselling author Mimi Matthews writes both historical nonfiction and award-winning proper Victorian romances. Her novels have received starred reviews in *Library Journal* and *Publishers Weekly*, and her articles have been featured on the *Victorian Web*, the *Journal of Victorian Culture*, and in syndication at *BUST Magazine*. In her other life, Mimi is an attorney. She resides in California with her family, which includes a retired Andalusian dressage horse, a Sheltie, and two Siamese cats.

To learn more, please visit

WWW.MIMIMATTHEWS.COM

OTHER TITLES BY
Mimi Matthews

NON-FICTION

The Pug Who Bit Napoleon
Animal Tales of the 18th and 19th Centuries

A Victorian Lady's Guide to Fashion and Beauty

FICTION

The Lost Letter
A Victorian Romance

The Viscount and the Vicar's Daughter
A Victorian Romance

A Holiday By Gaslight
A Victorian Christmas Novella

The Work of Art
A Regency Romance

The Matrimonial Advertisement
Parish Orphans of Devon, Book 1

FICTION *(continued)*

A Modest Independence
Parish Orphans of Devon, Book 2

A Convenient Fiction
Parish Orphans of Devon, Book 3

The Winter Companion
Parish Orphans of Devon, Book 4

Gentleman Jim
A Regency Romance